AF673101

1000 KMs to Leadership

1000 KMs to Leadership

Mohit Chobey

INVINCIBLE PUBLISHERS

Published by
Invincible Publishers
201A, SAS Tower, Sector 38,
Gurugram – 122003
Phone: 01244034247, +91-9599667779
Web: www.invinciblepublishers.com

This book is a work of fiction. Names, characters, places and incidents are either the product of the author's imagination or are used fictitiously. Any resemblance to real persons, living or dead, or actual events or locations, is purely coincidental and the publisher does not hold responsibility for the same.

First Published in 2020
Copyright © Mohit Chobey
ISBN: 978-81-945481-0-2

All rights reserved.
The moral right of the author has been asserted.

Printed at: Thomson Press India Limited

This book or any portion thereof may not be reproduced or used in any manner whatsoever without the express written permission of the author except for the use of brief quotations in a book review of a scholarly journal.

This book is sold subject to the condition that it shall not, by way of trade or otherwise, be lent, resold, hired out, or otherwise circulated, without the publisher's prior consent, in any form of binding or cover other than that in which it is originally published.

FOREWORD

Have known Mohit since early 2003, when we first met as co-workers at Standard Chartered's Indian arm. Coming from outside the industry & relatively inexperienced, thanks to my role had the fortune of having a ringside view of bank's talent-pool across multiple functional domains, & with Mohit struck a unique chord. Fit, agile & spirited even then, it was always a good fun to be with this impulsive Rajput, who left a lasting imprint on his assignments & teams spread across Bangalore & Mumbai in those initial years of us knowing each other.

Lucidly recollect my early interactions with Mohit, in whom one could immediately sense as someone having exceptional self-belief & a deep-rooted conviction on all things that needed to be done, to fix all that was needed to be fixed, to set ourselves firmly on the course of glory. Very ambitious, passionate & always with a strong point of view. Still recall, Mohit's worldview then was always black or white. Any shades of grey, vagaries & ambiguities used to rattle him a lot.

Over the years, with Mohit getting experimental in his corporate career, and as I jumped headlong into my entrepreneurial pursuits, our face-to-face meetings moved to once a year kind of a frequency. Despite that, for some subliminal reason we stayed in touch, & have always cherished his infectious energy, a unique blend of the nonchalant, yet deeply empathetic attitude that always leaves you with a sense of intrigue & awe.

Mohit's foray into running happened during this time, which initially I considered to be another of his passionate, yet mercurial forays (happened at the same time as his handlebar moustache). To everyone's glee though surely to Roma's (Mohit's better half) mortification, he seems to have stuck solidly with both! Fascinatingly, his bottom-less passion for running over the years has evolved into something much deeper (what he calls his '*Meditation in Motion*'), the physicality of it as a metaphor to explore one's zeal & zest for life.

As this book beautifully unravels endearing insights into Mohit's self-discovery & a push for a meaningful life-purpose, it in parallel succinctly interplays his take on what it takes to be a multi-dimensional leader. In a distinctive manner 1000 Kms… provides us with compelling life's lessons, for us to embrace in our personal journeys. To open our mind to limitless possibilities. To bolster our resolve to pursue our infinite potential!

Gaurav Dublish

CEO & Co Founder Wildcraft

7th Sept 2020

AUTHOR'S NOTE

I had the privilege of having grown up across the country, traversing its length and breadth, courtesy my father being in the Armed Forces for a total of 38 years until his untimely demise. I had started my schooling in Jammu, then moved to Srinagar and later, to Delhi, Shillong and Jaipur. My experiences in different schools and surroundings helped me develop adaptability and love for the outdoors.

I was always into sports, but running had been drudgery for me, and any distance above a round of the school ground was typically out of syllabus! As a teenager, I was befuddled by the running routine of the troops of the Assam Regiment (our campus was in the midst of their circuit). Their routine had running distances of more than 10 km, and at speeds, I couldn't even think of matching after 400 metres. True to their Salutation of Tagra Raho (stay strong), they were grinding the distances with Nonchalance. Their uniqueness is not limited to the salutation, but equally demonstrated in their regimental Song of "Badluram ka Badan" ("Badluram's Body") Major M. T. Proktor created the song in honour of Rifleman Badluram, a soldier of the Assam Regiment of the British Indian Army who died while fighting against the Imperial Japanese Army in World War II. After Badluram's death, the quartermaster did not remove his name from the rations roster and the company continued to draw rations in Badluram's name. This extra ration helped the company survive through a siege when Japanese troops surrounded them during the Battle of Kohima and supplies were cut. Accordingly, the song was composed in Badluram's honour with the lyrics "Badluram's body is buried but we get his rations". This song rendition is done at the passing our parade of the newly recruited soldiers and is a sight for sore eyes. They seemed to belong to a different species. As time rolled by, I eventually stuck to racquet sports, especially Tennis and made a dent in my school team with it. Not graduating much further.

My college days rolled by, without much activity on the fitness front. However, when I entered B School, I found my interest in running to be emerging. It was more than a means to stay physically fit, as a way to disengage from the rigours of my studies. The intense study schedule, regular classes, research and studying for tests, relative scale grades; all left no time for recreation, even for simply putting on my shoes and going for a run in the campus. Anyhow, this did not deter me from running, be it late at night, sometimes at midnight in the campus. Though Gurgaon winters can be biting cold, it was mentally refreshing for me.

Corporate life was a different ball game, altogether. As I dived into it with fervour, I did not know what existed in me. Further, harrowed with my father's untimely demise, the work became cathartic for me to deal with the tragedy. As the years rolled by, I lived to work and my existence pivoted just around being the best in what I did professionally.

Life gives us signals for course correction, and we can decide to either ignore them, or latch on to them and pivot ourselves into new directions. I had one such prompting jolt when I was diagnosed with high Blood Pressure at the age of 29.

Having been given warning signals, I realigned my work schedule to start developing alternate anchors beyond my profession, including dallying into fitness. I wasn't neglecting my professional commitments, but rather making my life more holistic.

Over the years, as I got more engaged in my running journey, I realised that it helped me in curbing stress and disappointments. And as the journey progressed, I started experiencing moments of sheer joy which permeated across all my engagements. It helped me develop into a better person, step by step, or would rather say, mile by mile!

When I was running the Comrades Marathon, it struck me as to how much I had transformed, both physically and mentally. As I became leaner and calmer, I saw that benefits arose not only in my personal life but that of my professional too.

That was a turning point for me, to compel me to pen and share my journey of passion with others. I feel that there are insights from everyone's life for all readers. Mine is not merely for the runners or the senior executives, but for people from all walks of life looking to lead themselves and the people around them.

Leadership is not limited to formal roles, but it is more often demonstrated in informal settings. Structured leadership does hold sway, but in an ever-evolving world with nebulous structures in society and new-gen corporates shouldering responsibility, moving forward surely necessitates leadership skills and the associated traits in every stratum of working lifestyle.

It is difficult for me to separate my journey as an athlete from that of a Corporate leader because they are intertwined and have been captured in the same manner in the narrative.

While the Core of the story is pivoted around my running experience, the corporate learnings are also incorporated as they arise from a natural discourse of revelation of my career and life on the whole.

You may choose to skip the highlighted learnings to continue with the narrative of the story and come back to it later or continue to peruse it in the sequence shared. Though, just feel free to go with the flow of the book as growth and learning is never linear!

This is the first book in my 3-book series on Leadership. The book also gives you a peeking glimpse of my next endurance journey, albeit of a different kind, as the next milestone with much more engaging fervour!

Even though a management graduate, I am not a big fan of Management books. I believe they are too dry and fail to deliver the requisite message because they leave out the quintessential Human element. Unlike the sciences,

Management is an amalgamation of science and art, with hues of different real experiences. Also, in the absence of earnest stories, the true message delivery fails, since at last, we all are stories, ourselves.

I hope that you tread this journey of Running, Life and Leadership with as much Relish as I have had while writing it down.

I would be remiss if I did not mention the role my family has played in my endeavour to be a Corporate-Athlete. To my two sons Shaurya & Aryaman and my wife Roma, I extend a heartfelt thanks for being a part of my life and making this journey even more enthralling for me.

My parents DIG M L Chobey & Kamal Chobey have played a crucial role in helping me define my moral compass and the values I live by. I could not have asked for a better childhood and I am forever indebted to them, not merely as my parents but also the wonderful Human Beings they have been. As to my sisters Rooma & Anjali, their everlasting faith in me has made me a stronger and wiser person and to my brother Anshul for being a partner in my evolutionary journey. A special thanks to Tanmay Dubey, friend and guide, for helping me walk the last mile to Authorship.

And finally, I would like to thank the running fraternity who have been fellow travellers in this adventurous life journey.

CONTENTS

CHAPTER 1

THE FALL: MOUNTAINS OF SOUTH AFRICA AND THE PROMISE

Only 20 kms left to run…

I had been running for the past 8 hours across the hilly terrain with an army of 20,000 runners in the Province of Kwazulu Natal in South Africa.

I started the run from the historic town of Pietermaritzburg; made famous by the father of the Nation – Mohandas Karamchand Gandhi; he was thrown off the first-class compartment of a train in ***1893*** for being a non-white, little did the TC know that he was actually fanning the fire which would eventually burn the British rule, enough for it to pack its bags and leave India in 1947.

The terrain was gently sloping. It was an idyllic countryside town, with the rays of the sun enhancing its palette of colours including various shades of green. It might have been just my enhanced blood flow speaking this. Supporters lined up at both sides of the road and there was an air of festivity. Families had come out to cheer the horde of runners. Some spots were peppered with Cheer Girls, who were gyrating to heart-pumping music. You would easily mistake it for a Sunday Joy run. The atmosphere got into me and I stepped up the pace. I pressed further on the pedal, thinking euphorically that I would be finally finishing the "Comrades Marathon", a ***mere*** 90 km run in the hilly terrain between the towns of Pietermaritzburg and Durban.

As my pace picked up, so did my confidence and I soon started flying. It reminded me of the time I was parasailing. As the tow rope slowly starts getting your feet off the ground, you start realizing that it is not merely your body, but also the soul which soars I looked around and caught the eye of my fellow runners, exchanging smiles and words of motivation. There was an invisible, warm bond that got created. We may not have known each other but we were comrades in the journey– A journey across the valley of 1000 hills– The Drakensberg Mountains of South Africa. In all the euphoria, I failed to see the protruding Cat's-eye on the way, which abruptly halted my run with a thud. As I fell face down, bracing with my arms to prevent injury to my head and face, I thought it was just a matter of some mere bruises till I saw my shorts turning crimson red. The realisation hit me: I was bleeding! I could not believe it for some moments. Just a moment before, I was en route to scaling the peak of Everest and next, I was in Mariana's trench. Thoughts started rushing: Was this the end of the journey?

Would my long 1200 km running practice come to naught? At that precise moment, I recalled the words of my younger son, "Dad, please finish the race." We had just celebrated his 5th Birthday on the night I flew to South Africa for my tryst with the Ultimate Human Race. He was overjoyed to know that I had planned my departure in such a way so as to not miss the celebrations of his birthday, even though I knew it would give me a day less to recover from my Jet Lag and acclimatize to the local conditions. As the celebration was winding up and I picked him up in my arms, he looked at me earnestly and said those golden words. The intersection of love, adulation and expectation was too overwhelming for me and I had to choke back a tear. As I recalled that moment while lying on the hot tar road, a continent away; my eyes moistened up, my throat choked, thinking of my failed promise.

I couldn't even do this for my sons…

CHAPTER 2

EARLY CORPORATE LIFE: KNOWING THE FIELD

Let me tell you a bit about myself. I am a 40-year-old young man, trying to resolve the abrupt halt in my career, or maybe trying to come to terms with the midlife crisis. I am blessed with a beautiful wife and two loving sons. I have been a young achiever, professionally speaking; starting my professional career with an FMCG brand, scouring the hinterland in mini buses, jeeps and tempos as a part of my Management Training experience.

I have been to towns which remind one of Rampur from Sholay. On one such visit to a remote town in Rajasthan by the name of Lakheri, I actually thought that I had stepped back in time! The colourful spectacle of one lane market, with small shops selling household wares, street urchins playing with homemade accoutrements, was a sight for sore eyes. It lit up the rather barren landscape. One could also see many *Tongas* ferrying their passengers, and I couldn't hold back an urge to peek into each one of them passing by, expecting the "Dream Girl" to appear imminently. I expected the band of dacoits to engulf the market at any moment now. The town also had one of the trademark high water tanks. It raised my heart rate on a somewhat routine visit. I had been traversing the length and breadth of Rajasthan as part of my induction. Having widely travelled, my father being in the Army; every 2-3 years, we would be gallivanting from one city to the other. I had also been to towns which had 'Rail buses' as a mode of transport– A first for me. It's a bus shaped vehicle that runs on tracks, not unlike the trams; this one ran intercity, a distance of 60 km in the golden sands of the Thar Desert. Another town I visited was close to Sambhar Lake, which provides a tenth of the salt supply for India. Its water is so salty that taking a bath in it makes you feel even more unclean.

Coming from the sands of Rajasthan to the plains of western UP, there is a town by the name of Muzaffarnagar. This town has the distinction of proudly proclaiming the highest crime rate in India. No wonder my daily sojourns with the local sales distributor into the countryside used to come to an abrupt halt at 6 pm and we were almost back to town every time before darkness engulfed us. I used to question my distributor, "Why would anybody want to loot a van full of batteries and tea?" His stoic reticence answered more than it hid, but I guess I was a bit wet behind the ears to encompass the wisdom being passed on.

As I traversed the country across the states of UP, Rajasthan & Bengal, it dawned on me as to why the FMCG companies include this as a part of the Training stint. Being aware of your ground realities is paramount to being successful, agnostic of the vocation.

I have travelled to 22 states, mostly for work and can say with confidence that I have travelled to *Bharat* and not merely to *India*. These journeys and experiences have been instrumental in shaping me as a person and a professional. Other than these, my voracious reading habit and upbringing have brought me to where I am today. But nothing has moulded my character or helped me become a better, rounded and competent leader the way Endurance running has done for me. I started inexperienced, wide-eyed in my career, with a wistful ambition of scaling heights which the icons before me had scaled. But eventually, I realised it is important to know the ground realities first-hand to know what's happening.

My humble beginning into running was sparked by a trekking expedition with my brother to Pindari Glacier. I was seeking salvation in the bosom of the Himalayas to tide over an interruption in my career; much to the chagrin of my wife, given that I would be inaccessible for days. In the current time, if you are not having an online presence, it's akin to *Harakiri*! In those days, just a mobile was sufficient to keep in touch with friends and family. Terms like 'Facebook Friends' and 'Instagram profile' were still to evolve. 'Tik-Tok' was merely the sound of the old clocks in ancestral homes. The terrain I was travelling to did not have the Mobile towers. In modern terms, I would be off the grid.

I have faced professional setbacks more than my fair share— it might have been something to do with my personality or merely being at the wrong place at the wrong time. While I have endeavoured to cross these professional chasms with a stoic approach and nonchalance in my initial years, later, in my subsequent years, traits developed and enhanced; while training for endurance running helped me integrate them better with my life and professional journey.

A long-distance runner will fail many times, sometimes due to injury, sometimes due to lack of practice, or merely because of inappropriate nutrition. I have had days when only running a half marathon (~21 km) seemed like a herculean task.

Why do we expect our careers to be smooth with no hiccups, failures or setbacks? The dynamics of the professional world are even more unpredictable and the more challenging responsibilities we undertake, the more are the chances of not being successful. Even Steve Jobs was sacked from the company which he had created from scratch; only to rise again and create a Masterpiece like Pixar.

Setbacks are integral to growth, and it's up to us if we want to institutionalize them as failures.

More often than not, growth encounters instability*. Be aware of it and respond, don't react. Often the difference shows when we allow some time to pass and let the emotions settle down, thus allowing us to have an objective view.*

CHAPTER 3

THE PINDARI SAGA

Life Lessons & Leadership styles

Anyway, let's get back to my time in Pindari and the trigger for endurance running. It is an absolutely scenic trek, to say the least. The Pindari Glacier is in the upper reaches of the Kumaon Himalayas, to the southeast of Nanda Devi and Nanda Kot, the two majestic mountains. The glacier is about three kilometres long and 365 meters wide and gives rise to the Pindar River, which meets Alakananda at Karnaprayag in the Garhwal district. During the trek, you get to see various shades of the high-altitude vegetation. Like the deodars with their towering hulks, standing like sentinels of the Mountains.

Himalayan vegetation varies according to both, altitude and climatic conditions. The Deodars give way to temperate forests in the middle altitudes. Higher up, coniferous, sub-alpine, and alpine forests spring up. Curled up on the laps of Kumaon Himalayas, the trek route to the magnificent Pindari Glacier is adorned by lush rhododendron forests and some rarely seen varieties of flora and fauna. These finally give way to alpine grasslands and high-altitude meadows or the Bugyals. The Bugyals funnel the clouds as if providing them a path to replenish the parched earth in the plains below. If you are lucky, you may find a herd of sheep grazing in the Bugyals. And from a distance, they resemble wisps of snow dispersed on the meadow.

They are followed by scrublands, which lead up to the permanent snowline. Each kind of vegetation provides a distinct character to the surroundings. You see a varied colour palette as you gain altitude, punctuated with the mesmerizing sound of the streams, fed by crystalline water of the melting snow. The Himalayas boast of one-tenth of the plant species found globally– enough to gaze around with wonder and joy. The lower reaches have a sprinkling of the villages nestled in the folds of the mountains. They remind you of a picture postcard.

The distinct vegetation you see there includes the seasonal flowers which bloom once in a year for a week just after the snow melts and are fed by the multitude of streams that spring up.

The majesty of the mountains is a sight to behold, with various shades of grey co-mingling with the snow-capped ones. The morning sun was falling on the peaks, making them look like shimmering gold cascaded from the heavens.

The Trek starts from a small town called Bageshwar in Uttrakhand. It's an idyllic town with the river "Gomti" flowing next to it. The closest railhead is at Kathgodam, a picturesque railway station a mere 200 km away. It has hills in close vicinity on both sides of the tracks and has the massive mountain ranges right in front with snow shimmering golden in the morning sun. We had taken the overnight train from Delhi Railway station amongst the hustle-bustle and stifling heat. As the train commenced the overnight journey, our minds too started climbing the mountains in earnest, causing a bit of a hiccup in going to sleep. The train arrived at Kathgodam the next morning, giving a glimpse of the majestic mountains ahead. However, in my haste to commence the journey, I lost my wallet. Fair amount of cash, my credit cards, and driving license were recklessly sacrificed for the sake of wanting to reach my destination as soon as possible.

Too often, I have found haste an impediment to meaningful progression and even, more so in running.

It has been a life lesson for me…Think before you act.

In our haste to achieve our distant goals or sometimes for other such reasons, we end up pushing our body too much and too fast– Resulting in injuries and a painful recovery period. All that speed goes for a toss and we possibly go a step behind from where we started our "speedy" journey.

In my leadership assignments spanning more than a decade, it was haste and impatience which formed my Achilles heel and dare I say for many of the other leaders too.

In our ambitions, we end up missing the ground reality in the hope of finding early Nirvana, often ignoring the environment and organisational capabilities.

An organisation cannot merely deliver because the leadership has ambitious targets. It delivers because the organisational capacity has been accordingly built and directed.

This often has to do with organisational cultures, a nebulous term for many, except the few who see the organisation as a living breathing creature having its own character and its strengths and weaknesses. It evolves like a child, from a Start-up with nimble footedness navigating in its immediate world with a speed and fervour which the adults merely ignore.

Based on success and milestone achievements, the character evolves. It is initially a reflection of the Founder/s and as the pace picks up, new feathers are added to the cap. It needs to evolve into a mature yet fit and agile organisation. It is often at this stage of a start-up when the scale is achieved while the character still has shades of the founder.

The question which begets answering is: Is it time for the organisational character to out shadow the Founder/s? The smart ones evolve their style to mature in tandem with the organisation's growth, whereas some allow their "egos" to direct the organisation as "they" deem it to be correct; often ignoring the external environment.

The one learning for me is: Leadership styles need to evolve based on the organisation's journeys, for the leaders to be relevant to the organisation else, sooner or later they shall be cast aside. In my handling of teams both big and small, I had to change my driving style; some of it was sheer maturing of the wine whereas, the other was based on the kind of resources available for each organisation. No single style fits all situations. Even if you are leading teams in the same organisation for an extended period, as the new crop of team members come in and the workforce grows, adapting to new styles becomes a necessity. This is akin to Situational Leadership.

The fundamental principle of the situational leadership model is that there is no single "best" style of leadership. Effective leadership is task-relevant, and the most successful leaders are those who adapt their leadership style to the *performance readiness* (ability and willingness) of the individual or group they are attempting to lead or influence. Effective leadership varies, not only with the person or group which is being influenced, but it also depends on the task, job, or function that needs to be accomplished.

Intrinsic to any leadership style is to be a "part of the team" and not merely being on top of the team. Leadership does not necessitate a one-way direction setting, but requires a healthy two-way interaction.

...The destination was the Glacier of Pindari, scenic and beautiful but also a testament to Global warming. I thought, next time I should take the Hallowed US President for the trip. You can see the shrinkage of the glacier. It has melted right before our eyes, to a dwarfed version of its earlier glory, yet mesmerizing still the same. This trek is around 90 km over a mountainous region and takes over 5 days.

The first day is a relatively short yet steep climb to a village called "Loharkhet", which we reached by afternoon. After a hearty lunch and an afternoon siesta, we headed for the village and explored the rustic, untouched beauty of the village, chiming with the sounds of the village kids playing cricket. The second most impactful imprint the British rule has left for us is the game of cricket, only behind the widespread use of the English Language. Dare I say, Indians have left the British behind in both faculties.

The second day was a stiff climb followed by a long walk, and my youthful energy was sapped to the core. This was the era in which my professional career left very little time for anything else. Fitness was a distant priority. I still hit the gym and swam a couple of times a week, but those were merely maintenance activities. I had not really invested in my health, the one thing which shows immediate results and provides long term benefits. Each day was an approximate trek between 12 -20 km, based on the next pit stop to rest the body and recharge the soul.

CHAPTER 4

THE PINDARI SAGA 2

Questioning your Existence

I have always found Mountains refreshing and regenerative not just for my mind and body, but also for my soul. They have ended up transforming me and made me delve into the inner recesses of my thoughts, navigating the quintessential questions of my existence and the meaning of it: Who am I in this large universe? As you stand in the shadow of the towering giants, you wonder at your insignificant presence, a mere blip. What would happen to the universe if you ceased to exist? Your absence would not even change a comma in the longest epic poem, the "Mahabharata". Its most extended version consists of over 100,000 *shlokas* or over 200,000 individual verse lines (each shloka is a couplet), and long prose passages. With about 1.8 million words in total, the *Mahabharata* is roughly ten times the length of the *Iliad* and the *Odyssey* combined, or about four times the length of the *Ramayana*.

Just when your self-worth is reaching a Nadir, you realise that for your immediate family, you are the whole book and maybe, for your children, the Universe itself. It brings a sense of realisation and balance in your mind, and helps you understand what the most important aspects of your life are.

These journeys open up the receptors. Treading the virgin pathways in the grasslands, you feel as if you are walking on a velvety green carpet, laid out especially for you and the gentle breeze caressing your skin, lulling your senses and you feel a strong urge to be enveloped by the mesmerising beauty all around. You look at the sky and wonder about what merely have you been seeing till now. Was everything before this experience merely a rehearsal of the real feel of life? The flora displays so many varied colours that your vocabulary feels stunted in describing them completely. It's an emotional rhapsody. The sheer beauty and the expanse of the terrain make you receptive to nature and the experiences around you. It's as if the layers of your defences have been lowered and you are experiencing nature and yourself naked, without any barriers or inhibitions.

We arrived at the base camp at the end of day two, having left our 20 other co-trekkers to walk back home. They had a notion that a trek is a family picnic and it was as if after having injured a mountain pony, they realised the gods were sending them a message. It was the right call for them. The trek does require a reasonable sturdiness of mind and body. After having a sumptuous meal that night, we settled for the night. And while electricity was not at hand, we were illuminated by the sky resplendent in its plethora of twinkling stars. My awareness of the Milky Way transcended into another level as I saw the galaxy in all its glory. As I gazed at the night sky, I was reminded of the mythological story of the two celestial Lovers, Vega and Altair. The story goes thus...

Vega was a celestial princess, a goddess of the sky. Immortal she may have been, yet she was weary as it seemed that she would live in eternity alone. One day Altair, a mortal, caught the eye of Vega. She descended from the heavens to greet him, and as they got to know each other she fell deeply in love. But when Vega's father finds out, he is enraged that his daughter would fall in love with a mere Mortal. His fury only grows when he discovers that Vega promised to bring Altair up to the heavens with her. In the cruelest of fashions, Vega's father grants the promise she made. The two lovers were placed in the sky as stars. So while they were both in heaven, they were not together. The great celestial river (known to us as the Milky Way) separated them. Yet each year on the 7th night of the 7th moon, a bridge of Magpies forms across the celestial river. Though it may be for one night a year, the two lovers are united then.

Given the plethora of stars, I bet the lovers didn't need the assistance of the magpies for the union; the stars were already doing it for them.

Day 3 was an early morning wake up at 4:30. We needed to start the journey early to be able to reach the glacier and walk after having our fill of the sights back to camp 2. It was a cloudy day and we had to walk with caution. The weather was pleasant but we were a bit disappointed by the blanket of fog and clouds as the peaks were not visible. Nor was the glacier visible. Although we could sense the presence of the Mighty mountains and the glacier with the gurgle of snow-fed streams providing music to the ears.

Luck is merely counted as a probability of chances, and some of us stack up higher on the possibilities. For some of us, getting things might be a bit tougher than for the others or significantly tougher, yet it is not something you can rue over. You might feel sorry for yourself while a very human emotion cannot overpower your senses. It has to be treated as such, that emotion is acknowledged and then cast aside. The "not so lucky ones" can either sulk or increase their chances of success by perseverance and hard work. No sooner than later, you will end up tilting the chances in your favour. Still, if nothing desirable occurs, it will surely build your character and give you a sense of fulfillment anyhow.

As the fog got denser, Bhatt sahib, our portly guide, with stamina equal to that of any soldier, advised us to turn around.

"Sir, there is no point in going further ahead. The Glacier will not be visible with the clouds so dense. Also, the weather is bound to turn bad and will become very cold when it rains. I would suggest we head back to base camp."

"Bhatt Sahib, we have come all the way from Bombay. Should some clouds stop us when we are so close to the destination?" I almost pleaded.

My brother chimed in, *"We can't go home and say that we reached within 2 km of our destination and then gave up!"*

In my heart, I knew it wasn't merely about seeing the glacier but more so about completing my objective; of reigniting my fire and filling my senses with confidence to take on the travails of corporate life and life in general.

I am not sure if Bhatt sahib was convinced by our words or by our fervent expressions, but with a nod, he started leading us the way on.

To quote Ralph Waldo Emerson,

"Do not follow where the path may lead. Go instead where there is no path and leave a trail."

This was as close to treading my own path as I could get, literally speaking.

We were hoping for the Glacier to unveil itself. And we were rewarded at last. The weather gods decided to shower their blessing and the low hanging clouds cleared away with the strong and icy winds which came our way. The Glacier was there in its full glory. Our senses feasted on its enthralling presence. After having basked in the glory of the Glacier and having feasted on our daily diet of potato and chapatis, we decided to head back. The taste of the potato felt refreshing, fresh from the village farms, and boiled in spring water with a sprinkling of salt. I would any day swap it for a nine-course meal. The flavours of natural food are superlative, impossible to replicate in urban settings. I was treated with delectable Rajma and Rice on the way back to Kathgodam at a beautiful locale called Binsar. Not even my mother's cooking stood a chance against that.

While coming up, we had noticed a small temple-like structure, which we felt was uninhabited. We decided to take a small detour and explore it on our way back. As we entered it, having left our footwear outside, we were surprised to find that it was also a dwelling. The interiors were dark and as we crossed the first small room into the main shrine, we were taken aback by the aura of that place. It seemed we had entered a holy domain and in the presence of a positive energy. The external environment too accentuated the feeling of being in a divine presence. No wonder the ancient sages sought the shelter of the mountains to attain nirvana. These lofty heights provided an abundance of solitude, beauty, and the enthralling presence of nature in all its glory. The next hour was spent in exchanging spiritual wisdom over a hot cuppa with the resident hermit. Succour for the soul and body. That night we slept well, in spite of the rarefied air and biting cold. A sense of accomplishment can do that to you, or maybe fatigue.

The next day was a long walk back to the Roadhead. Many take 2 days to do that, but we were high on *Josh* and decided to push ourselves. The trek took a long part of the day and we arrived near Loharkhet, all famished and tired. To top it all, transportation was nowhere to be seen; to take us back to the idyllic town of Bageshwar, which after so many days of solitude seemed like Birmingham to me, sans the Pubs.

In our endeavour to have a change of gastronomy and the pursuit of cold beer chugging down our throats, we walked another couple of hours and hailed the first available bus to Bageshwar. Often the reasons for motivation are very simple.

As I curled up in my sleeping bag, having downed a couple of bottles of chilled beer, I realised that my body had been pushed to the limit. There was also a sense of accomplishment as I had walked the whole duration of the trek with my 10 kg backpack. The much-needed stamp of approval for my youthfulness was granted by Mother Nature.

The need for positive strokes is a universal human requirement. It does not necessarily mean just awards or rewards, but can also mean a kind word spoken or an acknowledgment for a job well done. All of us draw energy from a sense of fulfilment of completing a responsibility or a challenge, and often that in itself provides us with a sense of gratification, but external acknowledgment works like icing on the cake and makes the success even sweeter. As we climb the totem pole of responsibility and leadership, these instances become rarer and rarer; as it gets a bit lonely at the top; however the need still exists and that is when peers and colleagues can make it a more rewarding experience. I have never walked out of a Board meeting with a pat on the back irrespective of the results; possibly it would make one a bit immune to the need for positive strokes, however, we cannot allow the same phenomenon to cascade down , and we have to be vigilant in ensuring the separation of the two engagements.

The way back to Kathgodam had the cantonment town of Almora as a stopover. There is always something special about these towns; one of the few things the British left as a legacy worth fawning over. The town is primarily pivoted around the cantonment. The cantonment blends in with the natural landscape and seems like an extension of the vivid beauty all around. It is merging of the wild and the manicured in perfect harmony.

With the objective achieved, the spirits healed and the mind focused, I arrived back home in Bombay with a sense of purpose and confidence- All ready to take on the world, reignite my health and stride forth in my professional challenges. Well, I was hoping for a hero's welcoming but was surprised by my wife's dressing down for being inaccessible for so many days. I was made to promise not to go for such ventures in the future. Anyway, time always heals.

CHAPTER 5

SOLVING PROBLEMS & THE JOYS OF LIFE

As chance would have it, I saw an advertisement for The Prestigious Mumbai Marathon on social media. My newfound confidence after traversing the Himalayas made me feel like a demigod. Eager to pick up the Gauntlet and wage battle. What was a mere 21 km of running compared to having trekked close to 100 km in high altitude?

After a week of retelling the story to my friends and family and basking in the glory of being a macho man, I decided to train in earnest for the forthcoming Mumbai Marathon. Even Demigods need to practice lest they forget their art.

The professional journey was marked with fine-tuning resumes, calling up consultants, professional connects and well-wishers. The trek had instilled a sense of confidence and purpose in me. I was no longer wallowing in the wrongfulness of fate and Machiavellian corporate politics.

Each of my interactions was being a reflection of striding forth with purpose. There were setbacks, as they always will be. I remember, once, I missed out on a coveted role as they found someone "more suited" to the role or maybe, they thought that I was "too young" for the assignment. Or, the mandate had gone in a different direction. This is an example of the expected pitfalls of working in the corporate world. The variables are dynamic and will not be controllable; however, what is actually controllable is our effort and our mental attitude towards circumstances.

We need to remind ourselves that the world is viewed by each one of us with a filter, which has evolved over the years based on our experiences, our learning, and to some extent, our genetics. What I view and what you view will always be different. The world is merely a mirror of our vision polarised by our minds.

As the running journey was unfolding, I was encountering a fair share of hiccups.

The first realisations were,

- Trekking and long-distance running are not necessarily the same.
- True, you need to be fit; but for running, besides your skeletomuscular strength, you need to have a good pair of lungs.

I had started at a small scale; 5 km runs, taking up to 35-40 minutes to finish them right behind my apartment in Juhu (a suburb of Mumbai made famous by the iconic Amitabh Bachchan) 1 km loops. If you are clear about your objective, you will anyhow find a way to achieve it. Here I was, practicing for a half marathon in a 1 km loop. No long winding roads, no flora to match the grandiose of a Trek, no sound of the gurgling stream with the nectar of the gods flowing through them; just a tar road and my running shoes. Grinding it day in and day out.

It's not how badly you want something, but how much hard work you are willing to put in it.

Takes me to my epiphanies:

* Are YOU SOLVING problems or
  » Merely trying to complete a task?
* Are you owning up to the responsibility or
  » Giving up at the first obstacle you encounter?
* Will you find reasons for failure or
  » Be Actionable for the solution?

These are fundamental traits for being successful. In most of the leaders I have reported to or who have reported to me, I have seen this fundamental difference; *their keenness to take up the load on their shoulders without mollycoddling their team and finding newer and innovative ways to stride forward.* They put stiff targets for the team, yet *participate in meaningful conversations* and free-flow of ideas from the team to recalibrate the strategy or change milestones if so required.

In the long run, they are more successful leaders, as they don't create a gap between themselves and the team.

During the training period, I eventually picked up a reasonably remunerative job, handling sales and marketing for a financial services organization. My days became more hectic with a higher commute time to my new job. People who stay in Bombay can understand the concept of commute time better than people in other cities, although Bangalore is fervently trying to dethrone Bombay in most time-taking commute. But I couldn't shortchange my quest to run the half marathon. I had a rep to protect.

Mornings were dedicated to dropping my younger son to school and then scooting to the office. It was highly gratifying to be able to spend those precious moments with him early in the morning before I hit the corporate treadmill. It meant going in the direction opposite to that of my workplace before heading back to work. Often our most memorable moments require us to stretch because these moments do not merely give us pleasure but wholesome happiness difficult to replicate.

Research shows that our most gratifying moments have little to do with the procurement of worldly goods and more to do with experiences. The current environment breeds in us a habit of buying stuff to be happy. Life in the 21st century is a fast-paced, consumer-oriented experience where the media surrounds us at all times enforcing the idea that happiness is a matter of buying the perfect house, driving the best car, wearing the trendiest clothes and posting status updates on the latest high-tech devices. While buying a new gadget or the first drive in a new car may be satisfying or thrilling for a short while, this thrill usually fades away and we find ourselves back in the same place seeking the next purchase to keep the recurrent loop going.

Recent research conducted found that people who spent money on experiences rather than material items were happier and felt the money was better spent. The thrill of purchasing things fades quickly but the joy and memories of experiences, from epic adventures to short encounters, can last a lifetime.

My most memorable assignments had little to do with compensation and more to do with the quality of the work I was doing and the environment I was working in. It is challenging to work in a toxic environment or with a toxicsupervisor, as the money cannot offset the energies going into managing him/her. At the same time, it's true that we may have to endure managing these situations for a period so that we get clarity on our destination and a sound strategy to arrive at that. There is nothing wrong with managing yourself during unfavourable conditions, provided you are clear about what is the eventual goal. Discomfort often can be a precursor to transformation!

The routine didn't stop. It took an effort to reach home at 8 in the night and hit the road by 8:30. The first kilometre was an arduous task, and the mind was a bit tired. The body more so, but as I got settled into my stride, I started experiencing a metamorphosis. I started experiencing euphoria as my pace fell in place; I realized what it meant to be a runner. As the sweat cascaded down my face, it replaced my fatigue with a euphoria.

I started stepping out more on weekends, and typically those runs were on Juhu beach, meandering through the throng of humanity, all itching to capture a piece of the sea and the vista. Some of my best races on the beach have been during the monsoons when the rain rejuvenates you with each step taken, with the background symphony of the waves crashing on the coast, untarnished by the human voice. Nature in all its unfettered glory.

Came the D-day of Mumbai Marathon, and I was ready to spar. The event was a sight to behold. It had taken Marathon running to a whole new level in India. The setup, the lights and the vibrant music were enough to pump up the runners. They were a whole new breed of runners evangelising a country not known primarily for sports barring a few.

Along with 1000 other runners (those days, it was still an “elite sport”), I was all set and ready at the starting line. We were waiting with bated breaths. Our first encounter with the distance, the mega-scale of the event, especially as a new shred of exploration of this vast field. The streets were lined up with onlookers and supporters. Something which rarely happens in the Maximum city. And then, as the shot rang out, loud and clear, we shot off. The strong runners started the run in haste, with their long strides grinding the tarmac as they leapt towards the course. There were others, like me, who had ventured to take on the challenge for the first time, careful in their strides at a controlled pace. The only pact I had made with myself was that I would finish the course without taking any walking breaks unless running up Peddar road became too herculean a task. This short stretch of road would arise like the Lochness monster around the 16 km mark for us, as a 1.5 km steep hill, strategically placed to test the mettle of the runners. It would not only test our lungs and legs, our resolves too. Little did I know that a few years down the line, Peddar road would look like a road bump in comparison.

I have often seen in life that transformation happens more because of the changing external environment and challenging situations; very few are self-motivated and evolved enough to register the need for change and then execute it with rigour.

We constantly need challenges to explore our potential; else we may merely end up becoming footnotes in our own autobiography, having failed to live up to our fullest potential.

Defining Success: What is the Metric?

Our success and failures are limited to our context and our domain. We win sometimes, which seems like conquering Everest and experience losses sometimes, which take us to an emotional abyss but may pale in comparison to a different situation or a different time or for a different person. At the end of the day, each one of us is alone in our life journey and while relative recognition may have its place in the scheme of things, in our life journey what really matters is what we are using as our individual yardstick. Are we living our lives or merely benchmarking ourselves against someone else who may have a completely different narrative?

That day was all about achieving my milestone of Conquering the Half Marathon. Seems ironic, I was merely conquering half of something, but that day it was a journey of a lifetime for me.

The Euphoria I experienced in completing the half marathon is difficult to transcribe into words. I had crossed the Rubicon. I was a runner now. And I loved it. Though, it was just the start of a lifelong affair.

To me, running had become **"Meditation in Motion"**[R]. It had become a default setting in my life.

Rain or shine, good day or bad day, joy or sorrow, I had to run. It made me feel alive, beyond just existing. When I run, I fly... I soar beyond my physical limitations. I experience each breath; I hear the sound of my heart beating to the rhythm of my legs. I experience each pore of my body... my cells come alive. My spirit soars and watches the world beneath with wonder and joy. I reach Nirvana.

CHAPTER 6

BACK ON MY FEET: WINSTON PARK, SOUTH AFRICA

I gingerly got up on my feet, brushing away the dust and grime, realising that the injury is not severe. I had merely suffered some bruises and a cut that was not bleeding profusely. A smile spread across my face. I was still in the race. I could still keep my word. As other runners passed by, commiserating at my fall, they were bewildered to see my beaming face. Having come so close to losing out on my dream, I was in seventh heaven to have evaded serious injury; there were no broken bones and my legs weren't rebelling.

The feeling of relief passed soon as it came– with a realisation that I have 20 more kilometres to complete before the victory dance could be undertaken. 'Could I still come true to my promise?' It was not just about a race, wasn't about feeling like a demigod, wasn't just about me anymore.

It was about my sons and me, and what life lessons they would take away from my success or failure. 'What lessons are there in store for me?' 'Will I end up becoming merely a better Athlete, or will this transform me as a person and as a Professional?' 'Will I be rationalizing my lack of success, or will I be taking life lessons?' I brooded in the time-lapse of some seconds. That day, I was keen to relish the nectar of victory. The question was, 'Did I have it in me, mentally and physically, to successfully finish the race in less than 12 hours to earn the Coveted Comrades Medal?'

The race has a history of breaking even the toughest and the best of athletes. Runners having completed the run ten times over a period may end up breaking down during the 11th. The distance and the terrain can be brutal to you. Also, its name is a misnomer. It's not a marathon. It's two marathons and much more, with about 90 km of running over hills which mimic mountains more and have little resemblance to hills.

The race was the idea of World War I veteran Vic Clapham, to commemorate the South African soldiers killed during the war. Clapham, who had endured a 2,700-kilometre route march through the sweltering German East Africa, wanted the memorial to be a unique test of the physical endurance of the entrants. The constitution of the race states that one of its primary aims is to "celebrate mankind's spirit over adversity".

The first run happened in 1921. The Comrades Marathon is an ultramarathon of approximately 89 kilometres, which is organised annually. It is the world's largest and oldest ultramarathon race. The direction of the race alternates each year between the "up" run (87 km), starting from Durban, and the "down" run (now 90.184 km), starting from Pietermaritzburg.

The spirit of the Comrades Marathon is said to be embodied by attributes of camaraderie, selflessness, dedication, perseverance, and ubuntu. Ubuntu is a Nguni Bantu term, meaning "humanity". It is often translated as "I am because we are" or "humanity towards others" or in Xhosa, "umntu ngumntu ngabantu," but is often used in a more philosophical sense to mean "the belief in a universal bond of sharing that connects all humanity."

Genesis

I was made aware of the race via a book I had read. I had yet to do a full marathon. And, here I was dreaming about running a 90 km race in another continent, and that too over an elevation gain of 7000 feet. To top it all, it had to be completed in a time of 12 hours, not a second more, because that implied a disqualification. It piqued my interest to the point that it became kind of an obsession for me.

Often in my work, I set up impossible goals, but the ones I could not achieve have at least made me think ***BIG*** and opened my mind to ***possibilities.***

As we progress further in life, we end up defining ourselves by our experiences and our immediate environment. To quite an extent, it helps us function well in that defined context but what it fails to do is discover possibilities.

A grounded mind with a soaring imagination can do wonders for us. It can show us new horizons without making us feel unanchored. Books and Travelling are two enablers, which help us roam the world with ever-evolving possibilities. All it takes is a bit of courage to scale new soaring heights.

We often need a push to unearth our potential. It can be from our spouse or partner, it can be from a coach, it can be from your boss or sometimes, from a friend. There is immense power in having a well-wisher who views you objectively for who you are, rather than what you think you are. My friend saw in me an athlete waiting to be unchained, and no sooner had I mentioned to him about my ambition to go for the Comrades marathon, than he started pushing me towards it. Even a fledgling eagle needs to be driven from the Nest perched precariously over the mountaintop, for it to take flight and relish the power of its wings. For me, the force beneath my wings was my colleague and friend for many years. I allowed him to pump me up into believing that I would graduate from running the half marathon to running the "Ultimate Human Race". He, himself, was a half marathoner, and he made me register along with him for the full version of the Bombay Marathon. He was putting his money where his mouth was.

I have managed large businesses and set them up from scratch. More often than not, it has been a positive influence of a colleague or a supervisor which has made me do the herculean tasks.

I had to go back to the drawing board. A marathon is not merely a multiple of the half version. During the marathon, you can encounter **"the wall"**. The much-dreaded word for any runner. The human body uses Glycogen as fuel for running. Each of us has decent reserves to go about doing our daily business. Typically, in a marathon, you encounter 'the beast' around the 32 km mark. It is that time in the race, when glycogen levels are so depleted that you may end up running sluggishly or transit into a walk, as there is no more energy left to run. This can be managed by primarily doing enough long runs before the day of actual competition to teach the body to store glycogen, and in the process also preparing the body to burn fat which is not a natural fuel to burn.

This also requires managing your nutrition: what to eat and drink during the run to ensure a successful and a strong finish. My training routine became more scientific, specific and disciplined. I could not rely on mere "**Josh**" anymore. While that may be sufficient for the half marathon, the graduation to the full version does require a much more strategic thought-through.

CHAPTER 7

MY FATHER, IN-LAW & MILIND SOMAN

Motivation to Keep Running

You would wonder what's common between the three of them?

Too many dissimilarities.

For one, they are from completely different professions.

While my father- and father-in-law have served the nation in the armed forces, Milind has provided much sought after warmth to the cockles of the heart of a generation of women and lately good health and athleticism to them courtesy Pinkathon, which incidentally I was associated with in the maiden year 2012, in my role as representatives of the associate sponsors.

I do get thrown into interesting situations courtesy my corporate responsibilities. The first such dalliance was the

Ms Bangalore contest all the way back in 2001. By the time the crowing of the contestants had to be done, all my seniors had left, under the glare of their partners. It was left to me to go up the dais and crown the beauties, which I did with aplomb. Only later did it occur to me that numbers could be exchanged, given that the age bracket was similar. I had got too engrossed in my professional responsibilities to focus on the personal ones. Kudos to my professionalism.

For the Pinkathon uninitiated, besides the fact that you see a horde of Ladies thronging the roads in gaiety once a year running varying distances in colourful attires, it is a platform for raising awareness of Breast Cancer and Women's fitness.

I was sharing the dais with a sought-after Movie star from the Kannada film industry who subsequently became a member of Parliament and Milind Soman. With the stage lit by two Luminaires, I was the side dish, but a dish none the same. Who knows what catches someone's fancy? Although I did get my fair share of second glances courtesy my handlebar moustache. This I believed held value in sandalwood country or nearabout; the event was in Bangalore. My moustache held me in good stead.

I hadn't started the day on the best of notes, courtesy the fact that I had to get up at an ungodly hour and pick up the "Star" from her home while she was still strolling around in her PJs and trying to get her dog back in her house. To top it all, she had locked herself out and I had to call upon my ancestral skills to climb up the balcony.

Before the race had even started, we were already racing to get to the venue in time besides running after the delinquent puppy. If I had rolled my eyes any further at my colleague, I think I would have empty sockets left. Anyway, after bundling the Puppy and the star in the house and the car respectively, drove with abandon to the venue. We had to do a run of our own to reach the dais. It was quite the sight, reminiscent of the Hindi movies, albeit the heroine was running along with me and not in slow motion. Before the eager crowd could register the presence of the running damsel and crowd her, I had safely ensconced her at the start point. To my relief there was a thanking note in Milind's eyes rather than a burning glare. His exposure to the film industry had placed him better to understand the nuances of the 'Stars.' I was still dangling my feet in them, reluctantly.

The event was quite a festival, albeit the runners keener to catch Milind's eye than to get about the business of running. Hats off to his stamina, not the running one which is indubitably noteworthy, but the ability to get himself clicked with the throng of women lining up to get him in the same frame. I bet his facial muscles have more work to do than his running ones. And you may change the locale, but the results will stack up just the same. Later, when he visited up north for another edition of the event, in my good old Gurgaon, the throng was equally boisterous and wanted to grab a piece of him and the action.

I noticed that this obsession was not limited to women in any specific age bracket. In one Mumbai Marathon Expo a day prior to the race I was being complimented by Milind for my handlebar moustache and we happened to click a snap in which he is holding them. He posted the photograph on Facebook & tagged me; little did I realise that this innocent gesture would throw my sister-in-law in Rhapsody. I got calls from her at ungodly hours from the shores 10,000 kms away to enquire, when Milind would be coming next to my place. It seems her next visit to India would be married off with his august presence at my house. At the other end of the spectrum was my niece who couldn't stop oohing and aahing over the photograph. Needless to say that his appeal is quite broad based.

You would again wonder, what has this to do with my father and my father-in-law?

They are much senior in age than Milind, the "Made in India" guy, although I always had eyes for his companions from Alisha Chinai, to Helen Brodie or for that matter the iconic Madhu Sapre. So, what, that they were senior in age to me. An appreciative eye does not discriminate based on age.

Although the first two are important senior figures in my life and have donned the Uniform for more than 3 decades, the heart throb of millions of women across age brackets has also played an important role in my running life.

But despite these dissimilarities there is a strong bond which binds the three gentlemen together.

There is another facet of Milind which is quite remarkable, and I was made aware of the same by none other than my Wife. It seems while seeing him run in the Mumbai marathon she could not take her eyes off his stride and his calves in particular. I wonder if the stride was added as an afterthought by her to assuage my feelings. This was news to me. And I can say it with all honesty my wife's observation powers leave a lot to be desired, and hence her comments about his calves were rather heavy on the heart for me no matter the thinly veiled distraction she had accompanied it with.

But not just Milind, but apparently even her father had the most charismatic calves or, so I am told. Although when I did continue to stare at them, my mother-in-law was a bit perturbed by my "Obhodro" behaviour, in non-Bengali terms, lecherous and ungentlemanly behaviour. On comparison with mine I thought I was the clear winner; to which I was informed that they were bulging pythons in his youth. Being a footballer and all that.

My father was a National level Hockey player and played for the Indian Army. Besides his robust body, the legs were a sight for sore eyes. I believe I had won that competition, with my pounding of the gravel day in and day out. Although he wasn't around when I de-facto crowned myself. But none can contest my claim, as far as my father is concerned. Rather, I have not put this up for debate.

So, you see, all three have one aspect in common. Their Bulging Calves.

But there is another one.

My wife has 3 sisters and her father lost all his hair with a household in which he was the only male. My soft corner towards him has its obvious reasons. What he lost in his plumage, he gained in unfettered affection from his daughters.

In my case I am blessed with two sisters and for reasons unknown to me, I was the sideshow in the house with adulation pouring over my sisters from my father in copious doses.

Having doused their respective daughters in sugar & honey, the two Gentlemen ended up earning the women's undiluted adulation and Love.

So, you see not merely the physical assets but being an adulated personality is what unites the three.

I am stumped from all angles

Well, as for me, I may have won the battle with my father but the war with my father-in-Law is still on, and since he is no more, it seems to be a non-winnable situation, as no matter how impressive my legs become, especially the calves, they will always be dwarfed by my wife's soaring imagination.

The things we do for Love.

Food for thought, my continued pursuance of Ultra distance running; what is the role of my Father and Father-In-law's calves?

Am I running the sport or merely trying to fill in my father's shoes and garner my Wife's attention?

CHAPTER 8

SIMILARITIES BETWEEN LIFE & RUNNING MARATHONS

A marathon, to some extent, is a simile to Life – For a marathon brings forth your life skills. It does not only mirror the critical life skills but also helps hone them.

A college in the US has launched a program called "Change through Challenge," in which the learning is pivoted around training for a marathon. It focuses on enhancing your life skills viz. Persistence, determination and grit by taking you through the marathon journey. The successful completion of the course happens when you finish a Full marathon. Because you only complete the race when you have honed and mastered your life skills.

Training for a marathon or an Ultramarathon is in itself a life journey. You can only finish it, if you have put in the effort. But the mere efforts are not sufficient. It is about discipline and rigour. It's also about putting in the effort when your mind and body refuse to respond. When your body is screaming with pain, but the mind pushes it, it makes it dig into the reserves of the body. It's about planning and diligent execution. It's about contingency planning; about researching your race conditions and understanding the environment thoroughly.

As I pushed forward in my pursuit of being counted among the top 1 % of athletes globally, I started to see changes in me. I became a bit calmer; reactions became responses and I delved further into self-reflection.

The D-day was approaching fast, barely 6 weeks to go, and I had to cross the Rubicon. This was the time when I started running more than 30 kilometres on my weekends. For completing a full marathon, you don't run the entire distance before the race, as it would tire your body and mind and take a reasonable amount of time to recover. Instead, you do progressively longer run-ups to 32-35 km before the event day to acclimatise your body and more importantly, develop your physical and mental prowess.

My first 30 km+ long run was a disaster. We started from The Oberoi hotel in Marine drive early in the morning and after traversing some loops, eventually headed back from the Worli dairy back to the starting point. By the time I crossed the 25 km mark, the sun was high, hot and humid and my pace had significantly reduced. By the time it was 28 km, I had transitioned to walking and running intermittently. This continued till the time I hit the Marine drive and had around 5 km more to finish the run. I had all but stopped running, on my last legs; with barely enough juice to walk back towards the hotel. Eventually, I completed the 35 Km run under 5 hours.

This was supposed to be my target time for completing the full marathon. Therun had gone horribly wrong. I hadn't finished it with a bang but rather a whimper.

I had just about 6 weeks to get my act into place. 'But what could I do?... Time to introspect.' Giving up on the run was not an option. 'What did I need to do more?' I sought the counsel of some seasoned runners and came up with a few answers. I wasn't having sufficient nutrition, and to top it, I was carrying maybe 7-8 kg of extra weight on the body. Not only did I have to get the nutrition formula into place, but I had to also reduce my weight without compromising my energy levels. I had a fulltime Leadership assignment, besides the fact that I had a family at home. Running was not my profession and I could not put everything on the back burner for my passion. There had to be a meaningful balance.

After much research, I settled on abdicating grain from my diet without compromising on my carbohydrate intake. I am aware of many programs that abhor carbohydrates and focus on high protein intake. I am no expert on nutrition and diet management, but I can tell you one thing: excess protein intake, besides causing other problems, eventually converts into fat. The fastest way to good health is balanced food habits topped up with good exercise. There is no shortcut to success. Eventually, all so-called shortcuts end up extending the journey much more than originally destined.

In this meandering, you don't merely lose out on time but most importantly, you are likely to miss the destination itself.

Four weeks into disciplined eating coupled with intense running workouts, I was 5 kg lighter. My confidence soared as did my spirits. Two weeks prior to the run, I could squeeze in only one more long run, as post the same I was to get into tapering mode– a term merely articulating the reduction in running time as well as the intensity– to ensure the body was relaxed and in fine fettle to take up the gauntlet of the marathon.

With trepidation, I embarked upon my last run, a distance of 32 odd kilometres. The route was more or less the same as the one I had covered four weeks back. This time it took me 3.5 hours to cross the finish line.

Exultation was an understatement.

I was inching closer to becoming a marathoner. To be part of the Global 1% elites.

While the elites were slated to start the run at 7:40 am, amateurs like me were slated for a 5:30 am start. I got up at 3:30 am to be picked up by my school friend sharp at 4:15, and was dropped near Victoria Terminus at 5 am. This architectural wonder is a historic terminal train station and a UNESCO World Heritage Site in Mumbai. One of the fascinating gothic buildings defining the character of South Mumbai.

We walked the rest of the way to the holding area, Azad Maidan, after emptying my bladder; I had ended up hydrating myself more than required. No matter how much you have prepared, you will always feel the nerves on your first run. So much so that I had not even got 5 hours of proper sleep.

As we lined up in our holding pens, I realised that the group had a fair bit of first-timers, reflected in the nervous laughter all around. Some had come as part of a group and were busy stretching their muscles and warming up for the upcoming run. Runners from the northern part of the country were finding the weather concerning. We had yet to start and the temperature was already in mid-twenties. Added to it was the ever-present humidity. Not ideal conditions for a marathon. Research, albeit done in western countries, suggests a perfect temperature of 10 degrees centigrade. The current conditions were akin to a furnace.

I shrugged my shoulders to get my muscles relaxed, and my mind focused. The hard part had been done. The gruelling training was over. It was time to stride forth and add another chapter in life annals.

The countdown had begun, and we started inching forward towards the start line. The starting point bathed in halogens with fast-paced music enhancing the explosive atmosphere.

The shot rang out and approximately 400 of us started our journey of 42.2 kilometres. The initial route included a fair bit of twist and turns coupled with the uneven road surface, heightening our senses even further. The rush of adrenaline coupled with the energy of the fellow runners and the supporting crowd can go to your head. I saw a couple of runners fall barely a kilometre in the race. I slowed down at a moderate pace to ensure the balance of mind and body. While the legs do the hard work of propelling the body forward, it's the mind which provides a semblance of balance and acts as the navigator of not merely the body, but also of your wandering thoughts. This was, after all, a 42.2 kilometre race, not a walk in the park.

Many may not be aware, but the first race is surrounded by a legend that dates back to 490 BCE. According to the legend, the Greek messenger, Pheidippides had to run from the battlefield in a place called Marathon to Athens to announce the defeat of the Persians. The distance of this epic run was 25 miles and according to legend, as soon as he had delivered the message, Pheidippides died of exhaustion. The original footrace was called a marathon in honour of the legend and as a result, it also covered 25 miles. The marathon ran from the original site in Marathon to the Olympic Stadium in the city of Athens.

For the next few years, the length of the marathon remained unchanged and it was officially forty kilometers, which calculates to just under 25 miles. However, in 1908, the Olympics were held in London and it was decided to set the course of the run from Windsor Castle to the Royal Box which was located at White City Stadium. This meant extending the course slightly to the current 26.2 miles and to keep the records straight and make it easier for the competitors to train, the distance of 26.2 miles was standardized in 1921.

I was hoping for a much better ending than the Greek messenger, Pheidippides. And it had Beer as an integral part of it.

I started at a steady pace and was, as usual, welcomed by the vivacity of the citizens, who had come out to support the runners early in the morning. The route was littered with Bands playing new numbers as well as some patriotic ones. Many corporates sponsor the run, and their stalls are choc a bloc with volunteers and sometimes, cheerleaders. It seems like a festival of running.

There were smiles, a sense of camaraderie and joy all around; the grimaces would start 25 km or so down the line. When injuries creep in, dehydration may set in or would merely hit the wall. I banished such thoughts and revelled in running on the traffic-free roads of marine drive, crossing Haji Ali, Worli sea face and eventually, *the Bandra sea link*; an army of runners making their way through on a patch of road, where pedestrians are not allowed barring this single day in the whole year.

I marched on with the galaxy of runners, eventually reaching the dreaded Peddar road, the 1.5 kilometres of a steep incline. Maybe the residents also knew it, because all through the climb, there were hundreds of supporters of all age brackets, including kids handing out candies and chocolates. The moment felt god sent. As you culminate the climb, the reference point being a bit ahead of the Jaslok hospital, you immediately get a descent, which should ideally be leveraged to increase the pace, but with the body having been battered for more than 4 hours, there isn't enough fuel to press the pedal!

This is followed by the turn around Babulnath temple and you are hit by the merciless rays of the sun. The next 5 km or so is all about running while trying to find patches of shade as a respite to cool down the body. Despite that you douse yourselves with litres of cold water, having ingested nothing less than 2 -3 litres of liquid, your body is on fire. Yet the flame to complete the run is more resilient and firmer in its objective. Nothing derails the run. Resilience pays off. The milestones are left behind one by one. Finally, I crossed the iconic “Jazz by the Bay”, a pizzeria where many an evening had been spent downing beer and chomping down on Pizzas; enjoying the pleasant breeze of the evening sea. I tried to banish the thoughts and get my mind back into the race. It was less than 2 km now for me to reach Nirvana. It seemed I had run a balanced race as I started overtaking some of the other runners who seemed to be at the far end of their energy. Sheer willpower was keeping them moving forward. They knew the pain and Grimaces were temporary, all banished when they would have been proudly displaying the finisher’s medal. I was tired and yet I picked up the pace, eager to get the coveted medal.

The end was near, and I could see the finish line. It said: 400 m left. I picked up my pace. I needed to finish with a bang and not a whimper.

I crossed the line in 4 hours and 50 minutes for my maiden full marathon. I was on top of the world. I had entered the Elite club, one of the few places money can’t buy.

The icing on the cake was when I saw my wife and all my friends waiting for me just beyond the finish line. They all came to me in a rush and I could see their beaming faces.

Their sense of pride was fuelling my self-worth. Satisfaction had multiplied.

Success is not merely the fulfilment of the goal; it is equally about the journey too. No goal will be worthy enough if the journey has not been lived and enjoyed thoroughly. You cannot merely bear the pain of the journey hoping to relish the joy of culmination. It must be lived, the pain and the pleasure, everything culminating into the grand finale.

For me, the grand finale celebration was at the watering hole of Cafe Mondegar, the iconic bar at Colaba Causeway adorned with the Murals of Mario Miranda. It had initially started in 1932 as an Irani café, later morphing into a restaurant and finally into a bar. It's one of the most famous watering holes of south Bombay. It seemed as if the whole of Bombay had descended at the cafe and on asking for the seating, we were brusquely informed that there was no seating available. On telling them that I had just run the marathon, I was informed that all were runners, to which I quipped that I had just finished the full marathon and was famished and thirsty. I then realised the value of that medal, when without much ado, seating for the 7 of us was arranged. Being a marathoner was still an 'elite club' thing back then.

I celebrated my evolution guzzling down beer with my friends and family. What more can one ask for?

CHAPTER 9

THE FALL & RISE OF ABHINANDAN

In times of adversity, my mind traverses back to 27th of February 2019. It's a date pinned on my radar, as the day Wing Commander Abhinandan Varthman created a history of sorts by downing a Pakistan Air Force F 16 with his vintage Mig 21 Bison (it was first manufactured in 1959 and production stopped some 35 years back). To give some perspective, it's like a Maruti 800 outpacing a Ferrari, given the technology divide.

As luck would have it, I had to go for some personal work to Kolkata the day after the event. For me it has always been a forbidding city, not necessarily because of the fact that my in-laws reside there.

I have been a business Leader for more than a decade & part of my job mandates travel across the country reviewing business, teams & Partners and sometimes to do the obligatory visit to the Mecca of the In-laws. It had been an uneventful flight, although I have had my fair share of flights brimming with excitement. From a bird hit, to a cracked cockpit glass, to flying over volcanic ash and plummeting like a rock. Not to mention the various take offs and landings at Bombay in Monsoons. Akin to roller coaster rides.

One such interesting flight was from Singapore to Mumbai. There had been a volcanic eruption in Sumatra, a few days back on the lines of the Iceland one. My elder son, forever the doomsayer, had questioned my wisdom of flying to Indonesia in these troubled times. I had replied with some petulance that I was going to Jakarta, which is in Java whereas the eruption had occurred in Sumatra. I had forgotten my Geography in my haste to be proven right. As we headed back on the flight from Singapore to Bombay, I was being serenaded by good wine and food in the Business class cabin not to mention the charming hostesses. Out of nowhere the ride became bumpy, and the pilot chimed in that we were encountering volcanic ash, and that all services were suspended. It struck me then, that flight path is over Sumatra and my son, decades younger to me, had been right all along. Before the air hostess could implement the Pilot's instructions, I had charmed my way into getting myself a couple of bottles of the wine, nectar at that moment of time; To at least go down while flying high. Eventually the flight soared and so did my spirits, sufficiently lubricated by the wine. It was the wind beneath my wings.

Anyway, as we were nearing the end of the Kolkata flight, I walked down the aisle to go for a bio break, more a habit than a biological need. You end up developing some patterns. Like booking the aisle seat to, or to ensure availability of your favourite newspapers. Even the toilet schedule ends up becoming a habit, bolstered by the need to stretch your legs. While waiting for the toilet to be vacant, the fasten seat belt sign came on. On enquiring from the hostess, she confirmed my premise that we were due for landing and to hurry with my business and get back to my seat. No cause of alarm.

I was patiently waiting for the toilet to be vacant before I felt a shudder. Which soon became a violent shake down, as I was thrown off my feet landing on the floor. The aircraft was not merely plummeting but shaking vigorously like a rag doll in the hands of an over excited kid. My mind was still processing the change of events, that I felt a warm sensation in my pants. As I sought to check the source, I found a trail of liquid emanating from my crotch; was suitably relieved to know it was merely the coffee seeping into my pants from the overturned cart. It had been as badly impacted by the G Force as I was. The contents scattered all over the aisle, and the liquids seeping up my attire.

The Air hostess handling the cart was tossed aside, banging into the rear exit. I was hoping for her sake that the door didn't fly open. In such times, the mind takes a detour from rational thinking. The other hostess was buckled up in her seat. As I tried to get up the G force kept me pinned to the floor. I manoeuvred myself between the two toilets with my back anchored against the door of one and my feet pushing into the other. In this melee, the occupants of the toilets tried to rush their way out, into perceived safety, only to be blocked by the full force of my body anchored in the compact space. I could have shouted a few expletives but was restrained by the feminine company all around, and in distress. Also, I needed the occupants' cooperation, and going to my north Indian language roots may not have done the trick. I was closer to the city of the Bhadralok than my Jat & Gujjar brethren of my new Karmabhoomi, Gurgaon.

The other hostess was goading me to get up and sit in the vacant seat beside her; no one had pleaded for my companionship so fervently and my motivation to sit beside her was at its peak, but despite the dual motivation, I was still losing the battle to gravity. Damn the G Force. It took all my strength to stay in the same position as the Aircraft continued its downward spiral and I kept gazing at the beckoning air Hostess.

As I lay sprawled, despite the obvious distraction, my mind went to the events of the previous day; when after having downed an F 16 Wing Commander Abhinandan had bailed out at 20,000 feet. In the Aircraft, an ejection seat or ejector seat is a system designed to rescue the pilot in an emergency. In most designs, the seat is propelled out of the aircraft by an explosive charge or rocket motor, carrying the pilot with it. The Pilots are ejected with a G force between 12 to 20. As such, the Pilots face serious challenges in the unfortunate scenario, they have to eject. Spine fractures are a common sequela of combat aircraft ejections.

Ejection and landing are the two events when a fighter pilot can sustain a spine fracture or worse.

Not only did Wing Commander Abhinandan eject at such a high altitude but also landed in enemy territory, surrounded by a crowd eager to Lynch him. Still maintaining his bearings & composure. Whereas, what we were experiencing was merely the retreating cyclonic storm which had visited Kolkata a few days back and was making a last pitch to rankle our nerves. It did rankle and more. Many in the plane had deposited the sumptuous meals into the bags or splattered theirs and the co-passengers' seats. It was mayhem.

It put things in perspective, and a smile played upon my lips. At that moment, a fellow passenger turned around from his seat to see me adorning the messy floor with a smile, and the look of befuddlement which transpired across his face made me smile even more. He was thinking I had gone cuckoo, when apparently, we were hurtling towards disaster and here; I was thinking how small a discomfort I was going through vis- à-vis the brave Air warrior. I had to merely keep myself engaged within the aisle and stop myself from rolling like a football, whereas he had to make split seconds decision to bail out at 20,00 feet after having been hit by a sidewinder missile which travels at twice the speed of sound. In the sordid scenarios, only our moustaches had some resemblance.

Too many times we tend to exaggerate our challenges by failing to appreciate what others might be going through. The idea is not to belittle your struggles, but rather have an appropriate context of what you are going through and what all you are capable of. Too often we merely scratch the tip of our capabilities, allowing ourselves to be overwhelmed by situations magnified by our self-absorption. To be true to your capabilities, the ability to dispassionately appraise yourself is critical. It allows you an honest understanding of your strengths and weaknesses, the lack of awareness of which can play havoc with you as a person & as a professional.

I finally overcame the G force, propelled by the beckoning face and crawled to the comfort of the vacant air hostess seat, clambering on top of it, the seat I mean, only to realise that the seat belt was geared for the petite frame of the air hostess. After some struggle was able to get it across myself, and as the eye of the air hostess roved over my dishevelled state, I hurriedly explained the coffee mishap before incorrect perceptions could be formed.

As things calmed down a bit, I first checked the state of the other air hostess. She had also hoisted herself to safety and buckled up in her seat. She was smiling, and it was a sight for sore eyes; the level of composure she had displayed was exemplary. I unfastened myself and took to comforting the lady coming out of the toilet, clearly in a state of shock, barely able to utter anything coherent, leave alone have a conversation. After passing her a glass of water and muttering some platitudes, I moved back to my seat. As I walked back people were looking at me with befuddlement, poised like 007, I walked with elan despite my dishevelled clothing.

While walking back to my seat I realised the extraordinary learning I had undertaken in the most unlikely settings.

Desist from putting undue focus on your struggles and adversities, they may pale in comparison to what others are going through, but more importantly they may limit your capability to fly, and inhibit you from becoming the true self you deserve to be.

Do not allow yourself to become a footnote in your own Autobiography.

Focusing too much on our struggles and challenges is a sure shot way of limiting our capability to fly. Some of us may be evolved enough as individuals & professionals to bring about that change. But for many of us, we need to put our challenges in perspective to be able to see how insignificant they may be, and how they limit our capabilities to develop.

CHAPTER 10

THE TRANSFORMATION

Having conquered my first big summit, I relished the rest of the day with my wife and sons.

I didn't have any rest post my race as the very next day, I had a business review scheduled with the CEO of Asia Pacific.

I walked in bright and early with a spring in my stride and a smile on my face. I knew the conversation was not going to be easy. I had been dreading this conversation. And yet, I was in high spirits. I knew the answers but did not necessarily have the solutions yet. The organisation's top line was not growing on expected lines. On the other hand, costs were on an upward trajectory.

All in All, it was a recipe for disaster. Some firm calls had to be taken, tempered with logic, and some EQ. In spite of the upcoming challenging conversation, I was calm and composed.

The marathon had done something to me. It had brought about a sense of confidence and clarity. It had taught me to manage tough situations. To adapt to a changing environment and to dig in deep. The conversation was tough but logical, and had an imminent meaningful action plan. Nothing works like composure and reflection in managing difficult conversations. Because then, you allow logic to overwhelm emotions and personal stakes. Not only was I becoming a better runner but a better leader too.

And apparently, science and research were backing my transformation.

Physically Fit CEO, Financially Fit Corporation

That's the conclusion of researchers, who, using the completion of a marathon as a proxy for fitness, found that fit chief executives led more successful companies. After identifying CEOs of S&P 1500 companies who had completed a marathon in each year between 2001 and 2011, researchers found that the firms with top executives who had completed a marathon were valued 5 percent higher on average than those which had executives who had not. This merely converts to 1500 Billion USD.

This seems counter-intuitive. The professionals with the least free time and herculean responsibilities need to dedicate time to running marathons and endurance sports in general, which in itself is a big commitment. So then, why do they do it? And why is there its positive correlation with Organisation performance?

Part of the answer lies in the fact that Successful leaders don't count the hours; they make the hours count.

Successfully running a mid to large company/ a start-up is kind of like running a marathon:

Both require diligence, commitment, work ethic and strategy.

But does being a marathon runner make you a better leader?

A significant proportion of CXOs now incorporates running and exercising in their daily routine. They put themselves in challenging situations in their physical activities to not only get a tangible benefit, but also to provide themselves with "me" time and *space to reflect and meditate.*

As for me, this has moved beyond the sheer beauty of the whole process; it lifts my mind into a state of transcendence. Appreciation for my surroundings gets amplified as does the understanding of my mind and body.

It brings me into a state of Zanshin.

Zanshin in Japanese means "residual mind".

It refers to a state of relaxed awareness in which a practitioner of martial arts is wary of his surroundings before, during, and after attacks.

Familiar are the surroundings for CXOs.

"The new breed of CXOs don't just make time to run – they feel running is a cornerstone for success in all areas of life."

"Fitness moderates stress and increases cognitive and job performance. Thus, it should be relevant for CEOs as they face high levels of demands and responsibilities, particularly work stress and physical requirements."

A CEO typically faces daunting challenges, be it exponential revenue growth, the drastic improvement in margins, or simply managing shareholders. Each task in itself is a full-time job and to be able to manage all these at the same time can overwhelm anyone.

The trick lies in breaking it into ***chewable chunks***. Even if it's only about focusing on the building blocks and allowing periodic milestone appraisal, it all adds up to the bigger picture without weighing down the ability to shoulder the challenges.

Often in running marathons, we are racing against ourselves, pushing our mental and physical boundaries and in some rare moments, ***transcending into a meditative state***. There are distractions like, how well others are performing and 'Am I being left behind?' More often than not, the preparation for the race makes us much more aware of our capabilities and game plan.

While we may be seduced by the idea of going faster, we know that it will result in an early burnout and what was supposed to be a victorious triumph will turn into the dead man's walk.

Each organisation builds its capabilities, and more often than not, ***it takes time and commitment***. Competitors may race ahead of us, in the short term, but the true essence will come out as the field spreads.

Competitive edge and sustainable growth are not overnight phenomena. Successful CEOs realise this and focus their energies on creating "capability" rather than allowing themselves to be seduced by opportunistic growth.

One significant trait which gets nurtured in the process of preparing and running for marathons is the development of flexibility and adaptability.

Obstacles will arise during your race — you won't be able to prepare for all of them. The key to finishing the race strong lies in your response. Leaders are bound to make mistakes, but it's their ability to step back and evaluate the situation in a pragmatic manner which makes all the difference.

Running marathons and endurance races is so much like managing your life, personal and professional. You may not realise it but each step you take in your life is like a marathon you run.

What better way is there to simulate the conditions of life and the corporate life other than running a marathon and thereby, compressing your learning curve?

A study published in the HBR by a Performance psychologist, Jim Loehr and an author, Tony Schwartz under the heading, The Corporate Athlete, tries to uncover the correlation between top-performing athletes and their abilities as Corporate Executives. They believe that Management theorists have tried since long to unravel the mystery behind why some people break down under pressure whereas others flourish, with an approach that is defective. The approach has been limited to analysing the neck up, correlating high performance primarily to cognitive abilities. Some theorists have extended the correlation to EQ and to the spiritual dimension- how deeper values and a sense of purpose influence performance. However, no one has paid any focus to the physical capabilities. As per them, the ideal performing state can be achieved by the body, the emotions, the mind, and the spirit working in Harmony. Failure to address any of these aspects compromises performance. In effect, these leaders are akin to "corporate athletes".

Extensive research into sports science has defined the capacity to mobilize energy on demand as the foundation for the ideal performance state. Stress rather than being an impediment is actually a stimulus for growth. The problem is the absence of disciplined, intermittent recovery. As in sports, so in corporate life, the need to pause and recover is a recipe for a successful career.

I was getting back to the corporate rigmarole but I had a nagging pull towards the Comrades Marathon. It seemed like a Herculean task and yet, somewhat achievable. I felt if others could do it, what could stop me from ascending the totem pole of Long-distance running? In my friend's words of wisdom, running a marathon was like driving through the fog; you may not be able to see your destination but slowly and surely, the fog sets aside enough for the path to be visible, and before you realise it, you have reached the destination. I was trying hard to use the metaphor for Comrades, but every time the 90 km distance straddled with hills and an elevation of 7000 feet ended up choking my car's engine.

The next year came and went smoothly without much action on the running front. Though, a lot was happening professionally. The organisation was playing musical chairs with CEOs and we had a barrage of them. In such unstable times, many colleagues left for greener or other pastures. I continued toiling and was able to make a dent in the organisation's Asia Pacific leadership, being finally touted as the best Business Leader across the APAC region.

Corporate life can be more dramatic than Bollywood, sometimes. Barely had I got the smile off my face on being recognised in the APAC region when I was told that my role had become redundant. I walked out of the cabin with a stoic face and called up my wife, informing her that we were going out for lunch. She thought it was celebrating a new success. Midway during the meal, she finally asked me the reason for my celebratory mood; to which I replied, "I have been fired."

She was stunned at my diabolical behaviour, to which I responded by saying that my ability to live life and be happy cannot be dependent on the organisation's vagaries. I couldn't stop being happy just because I had encountered a tough situation.

We give too much focus to our pains and very little to our pleasure.

I am not sure if she was convinced with this thought of mine, but she definitely knew that I had changed. And I also knew that I had changed. And not merely changed, but evolved. Into a stronger person, an adept athlete, and a Holistic Leader. In my life now, the sport stopped being only as a means to physical fitness; it had morphed into a catalyst for emotional and spiritual evolution.

Mental resilience and strength are skills that you develop over the years.

It's not necessarily an inherited trait. All of us go through challenging times in our personal and professional lives sometime or the other. While the situations may be unique, the experiences are shared. For me, the most significant element in having a flexible approach to tough situations is to focus on what I can do, rather than what has happened.

The minute we change our focus, our thoughts get accordingly aligned and are focussed further on solving the problem. This often brings about an infusion of hope and consequently, positive energy; the Key ingredients in making us strong.

With the doors with my current organisation having been closed, another opportunity opened up with an organisation in Delhi from a different Industry. I had started my career in FMCG, moved to Two-wheelers, Banking, Insurance, and now was delving into a new domain. There was a mild flutter on leaving Bombay, my home for the past decade. But these were minor pangs which would be going away with time. In a way, I was looking forward to staying in Gurgaon and experiencing open spaces after having lived for long in the Sardine state of Bombay.

CHAPTER 11

THE ROAD TO COMRADES

Running in Gurgaon is not for the elite few; it seems the whole of the middle-aged crowd is on the roads day in and day out. The culture is vibrant for runners and athletes and is complemented by the Aravallis at the edge of the town. The Aravalli Range, an eroded stub of ancient mountains, is the oldest range of fold mountains in India. The natural history of the Aravalli Range dates back to times when the Indian Plate was separated from the Eurasian Plate by an ocean.

Unlike Bombay, you don't need to always look over your shoulder to see who will be banging into you. There are enough and more roads and trails, including some hilly tracks. All in all, a runner's paradise, except in the period from May to August when the weather roasts you! An early morning run is the only solution. The runs, sometimes, take you to rural Haryana, with a plethora of villages in the vicinity. Gurgaon is an interesting juxtaposition of the Ultra-modern, with its skyscraper malls and corporate hubs rubbing shoulders, with the rustic charm of the villages. The running sojourns give you a glimpse of rural India and bring about a refreshing new understanding of the same. The city also has a CRPF training camp for recruits in the vicinity. You can run in cadence with the recruits, along with the *Ustaads*, urging the recruits to bring up their pace. It's a great feeling seeing *Josh* of the recruits, especially of the women carrying their rifles and backpacks and running shoulder to shoulder with the running brigade. These guys can give you a run for the money. Further on are the Haryana armed police lines which can be a bit daunting on entering their premises, but on a lucky day, you can traverse your way to the forest area, resplendent with the calls of the wildlife. These are trails protected from the harsh sun by shadows of the overhanging flora.

From the CRPF to the Haryana armed police, the new recruits are on the move daily, early in the morning, treading the roads and trails of rural Haryana. Most military institutions have long-distance running as a critical ingredient in their training program. It doesn't matter how much weight you can carry or how good a shooter you are, if your running timings are not in the stipulated benchmarks, you fail to cut. The Para Special Forces of the Indian Army have a 100 km run as an integral part of the running program. It seems nothing depicts fortitude and character like long-distance running. The ability to dig into your physical and mental reserves; intrinsic to being a warrior and a leader. For the toughened army soldiers, earning the sought-after Red Beret requires the long-distance run to be finished. No matter what.

It is hypothesized that the success of the Human Race is because of its running prowess over Long distances. Most mammals can sprint faster than humans; having four legs gives them an advantage. But when it comes to long distances, humans can outrun almost any animal. Because we are cooled down by sweating rather than panting; we can stay cool at speeds and distances which would burn out other animals. As per scientists on a hot day, a human could even outrun a horse in a 26.2-mile marathon!

Why would evolution favour the distance runner? The prevailing theory is that endurance running allowed primitive humans to incorporate meat into their diet. They may have watched the sky for scavenging birds and then run long distances to reach a fresh kill and steal the meat from whichever animal they encountered first.

Another research suggests that before the development of slingshots or bows, early hunters engaged in persistence hunting, that is, chasing an animal for hours until it burns out, making it easy to kill at close range. A 2006 report documents persistence hunting among modern hunter-gatherers, including the Bushmen in Africa.

I didn't have to relocate to Africa.

I had to merely change gears while getting into the long-distance mode. Basically, it was about relearning the traits of my forefathers. The reasons for their success over other two-legged Mammals.

I had not only changed my city, my job and my industry but was on a course to change my marathoner tag with a "Comrades Finisher". I had taken the bold step of Registering for the Ultimate Human race right after I got back from another Soul cleansing trek to the Glacial Lake, Roopkund at an altitude of approximately 16,000 feet. Significant transformations in my life necessitate a period of reflection and course correction. I have often found that being close to Nature provides me that catalyst. It triggers in me the need to discover my boundaries and alter them.

Ever since I was a child, I was into sports; my natural inclination was to indulge in physical activities. And courtesy of my father, I had developed an affiliation towards tennis and was a good player of racquet games. He later introduced me to Golf but that Love affair passed away with his demise. Some experiences in our lives are wholesome not because of the setting or situations, but because of the company.

Besides Tennis and Golf, I was an avid viewer of the Olympics. The parade of nations with the athletes demonstrating prowess beyond my comprehension was something which enamoured me from early childhood.

The Olympic motto is the *hendiatris Citius, Altius, Fortius*, which is Latin for *"faster, higher, stronger"*. It was proposed by Pierre de Coubertin upon the creation of the International Olympic Committee in 1894.

Coubertin said "These three words represent a programme of moral beauty. The aesthetics of sport are intangible." The motto was introduced in 1924 at the Olympic Games in Paris.

The most important thing in the Olympic Games is not to win but to take part, just as the most crucial thing in life is ***not the triumph but the struggle***. The essential thing is not to have conquered but to have fought well.

These words have always inspired me, *and I know I may never compete in the Olympics, but I can strive to achieve the best I can be.*

At the end of the day, that's what each one of us can strive for, to reach our states of self-actualisation.

CHAPTER 12

ROOPKUND: ENIGMATIC GLACIAL LAKE

The pursuit of self-actualisation was once again undertaken; I had my brother towing along with me to the stark and spectacular beauty of the high mountains. The trek was of a very high difficulty level, but from being an infrequent gym attendee, I had graduated to being a full marathoner from my previous trek. So, I was quite confident about undertaking this one.

As we arrived at our railhead of Kathgodam once again, we felt as if we had come back to a long-lost friend. The journey from there to the base camp at Lohajung was a long and tiring one, though nature did its best to lift our spirits. As we arrived at base camp, we met an enthusiastic bunch of college pass-outs from Bangalore. Energy oozing out of each pore of theirs. The mood got contagious and after doing our registration, we headed to the local market. Well, it was hardly a market, as there were not more than a dozen shops in a single lane, guarded by the well-fed mountain dogs. They were a sight to behold, with their gleaming furs and robust bodies; which could have been mistaken for wolves.

The preparation of this trek had been a bit more intense, given that most of the trek would be at an altitude of more than 12,000 feet. We had been advised a regimen of high-altitude sickness tablets. The idea was to make our bodies less susceptible to altitude sickness. The air gets significantly thinner with altitude gain. At 10,000 feet, the available oxygen is 70% of that available at sea level. By the time we reached our destination, it would have been down to 50%. The impact can be from acute mountain sickness, resulting in headaches, nausea and disorientation or an extreme form when fluid gets filled up in the Lungs or worse, in the brain. We were well prepared mentally and hopefully, physically too.

It took us two days of hard trekking to reach the launching pad for Roopkund, called *Bhagwabhasa*. The route kindled the soul. The high-altitude lush meadows, with green carpeted grass bereft of trees, barring the hardiest, brought a sparkle to the eye. Most of the trek was above the tree line, yet it did not diminish the beauty of the landscape. The last part of the trek to Bhagwabhasa was eventful in more ways than one. To begin with, this particular patch had the steepest climb to Kalu Vinayak, an ancient temple. This temple is dedicated to Lord Vinayaka or Ganesha. This is made inside a small cave with small, flat pieces of stones, and inside it, there is placed an idol of Lord Ganesha made of black stone.

While ascending this climb, the weather had started taking a turn for the worse. The clouds had descended, and we had a tough time keeping ourselves on the trail. I had ended up being ahead of the leading group, though I did have our guide with me. As the trail got enveloped in thick fog, I lost sight of Bahadur, our guide. It was a surreal surrounding with a narrow path up the mountain and a steep fall on the other side. My senses were all keyed up and I was a bit nervous. After taking one of the umpteen turns, I was relieved to see Bahadur perched on a boulder at the end of the turn. I called him out in relief and was flummoxed when he didn't revert. Thinking that he might be a bit far off, I again called him out, a bit louder this time, only to hear my voice echoing back! This was beyond eerie and it reached a peak, as I reached closer to the boulder and found no one sitting on it. Almost on cue, the wind picked up and I could hear the valley come alive with the whistling sound of the wind. As if this wasn't enough, my mind wandered to the book by Ruskin Bond, "A Face in the Dark." It's about Mr. Oliver, an Anglo -Indian teacher, whose late evening stroll through the forest brings him face to face with a young boy's ghost, who doesn't have a face. And the scare doesn't end there; when the teacher seeks help from a watchman, he saw that he didn't have a face too. I was feeling like Mr. Oliver right now, though in his case, he was wandering within the vicinity of his house whereas I was delving into unknown territory...

My need to reach the temple became severely amplified and en route the rest of the walk, the name of the Lord didn't leave my lips. I gravitated between thinking about Lord Ganesha, within walking distance of providing salvation to me and my favoured deity of strength, Lord Hanuman. I wasn't leaving anything to chance as I chanted my mantras by rote. None too soon, I reached the temple, nothing less than a miracle for me given my recent bout of experience, and was joined by Bahadur who couldn't fathom the reason for my baleful look. My brother got a similar treatment from me when he made his presence felt. Had I not been in front of a Temple, a litany of expletives would have been flowing.

Having savoured the prasad, we proceeded to Bhagwabhasa, and encountered a terrain never seen by either of us. We felt as if we had reached the moon. There was not a blade of grass and boulders were strewn around as if a giant had played checkers with them. You could have shot any of the star trek movies here. A desolate alien environment. We reached the camp and just when we were downing our cuppa, the heavens opened up and pelted the ground relentlessly with stone sized hail. While we were thankful for having reached in time, our thoughts were with our co-trekkers, who would have been facing the full fury of the hail. Some of them started trickling in, wet and cold and with spirits a bit damp. Nothing which a hot cup of tea and a fire wouldn't take care of. However, as the last stragglers came in, we realised a couple of them were in bad shape. They were shaking uncontrollably, and it was clear that they were experiencing hypothermia. After taking off the wet clothes, they were wrapped in layers of warm clothing and sleeping bags. It took quite some time before their shaking stopped. However, they knew that they could not go any further. Experiencing Roopkund would be for another time.

The final ascent was slated to start at 4 am. It was dark and cold. We had spent a miserable night trying to catch some sleep in the biting cold. With 4 layers of clothing and been tucked in a sleeping bag with Fleece, I still lost the battle in keeping the cold out. It was below freezing point and the chilly wind made matters worse. On top of that, answering nature's call was an expedition in itself. Firstly, I had to navigate myself out of the crammed sleeping tent, jostling silently amid 3 of us packed like sardines. Then, I had to walk a reasonable distance to behind one of the boulders. By the time I got down to doing the business, I was panting like a dog.

On one such occasion when my brother was looking at relieving himself in the middle of the night, after losing the battle with his bladder, he ended up shaking the crammed tent so violently that I thought a wild animal had entered the tent. After all, this was prime territory for the mountain Leopard.

I have had a first-hand experience of the majesty and strength of the Leopard while driving back from the Ski resort of Auli to Haridwar. In the middle of the night, after having finished a sumptuous meal at a local Dhaba, our friend had braked the car to a hard stop, staring intently at the two red ambers looking at us with nonchalance in the shade of the towering deodars. After having given us a look over, satisfied that this meal wasn't easy to come by, the beast jumped to the ledge a mere 7 feet high, effortlessly. We remembered that trip as much for that feline as for the skiing done on the slopes, shimmering with fresh snow. I wasn't keen to have the encounter again, even with the protective enclosed cage of a car.

Though, South Africa had shown me that Elephants are to be feared more than the Big Cats. On a visit to a private game reserve, I was surprised to see that the parked Safari vehicle was a land rover jeep, without a hood over the passengers, and even the windscreen was folded down onto the bonnet. You couldn't feel more exposed. On top of that, my co-passengers comprised two ladies with their children. Gallantly, I sat in the front with our driver and guide, who was carrying a vintage gun, which I thought would be hard-pressed to shoot anything, leave alone a Lion. As we meandered in the park feasting our eyes on the fauna, we eventually came across a herd of elephants.

Having seen the rather gentle ones in my sojourns to my hometown of Jaipur, I was initially unfazed as they approached us. One Tusker, in particular, came to inspect us more closely, and our guide slowly started backing the car. The tusker picked up the pace and was soon charging at us. 6 tonnes of pachyderm charging at us, filled the complete panorama, and we were driving backwards at full pace because on one side was the jungle and the electrified fence on the other. In this melee, I picked up my courage and asked the guide at what speed we could move back the car.

Pat came to the reply, "40 km per hour". I ventured further and asked, "At what speed can the elephant run?" Without batting an eyelid, the guide said “40 kilometers an hour”. I was getting wary about his knowledge of the car or the Tusker; at that point in time, the math was getting a bit edgy.

Thankfully, after giving chase for a couple of minutes, it meandered into a nearby grove. After this chilling encounter, sitting in the open car with 5 lions lazing within 15 feet distance from the vehicle was a cakewalk.

Having come out of my reminiscing zone, I ventured towards the eating area. Morning breakfast was puri and aloo, munched down with gusto. The morning was equally eventful as one of the trekkers developed mountain sickness. In such a scenario, the only way to recover is to head for a lower altitude. The trekker was keen to continue, but eventually, sanity prevailed, and he headed for the bugyal, accompanied by a guide. Meanwhile, we were having a tough time navigating the trail. It had frozen over, and we had to be mindful of each step taken. This was a tough climb on a narrow trail.

I was keen to see the famed lake and hurried my pace, in step with the Lead guide. After a couple of hours of strenuous climbing, we reached the famous lake. For the uninitiated, this lake is host to around 300 skeletons from the medieval period, in pristine condition, courtesy the cold weather. Surprisingly, this didn’t bring about morbid thoughts, but more of curiosity and awe.

The lake top was frozen and it looked like a giant icing rink. As I was absorbed in the beauty of the lake, I was rudely jolted by a shout from one of the trekkers. He could not hold back his enthusiasm. The aftermath of the rambunctious call was the lake making a loud crackling sound and breaking off a chunk of its cover. The upheaval in the lake caused us to hurriedly back our steps into safety. The look from the lead guide was enough to kill, as he walked purposefully towards the troublemaker.

The rest of the group arrived, and we were served with a sumptuous meal. Having our bellies full and our eyes feasted, we were ready to head back to base camp 2. But that was not to be, as we had been blessed with remarkable weather and made good time reaching the lake; our guide decided that we should climb up higher to JunarGali, right in the cradle of the mountain peaks of Trishul and Nandaghunti, both peaks comfortably crossing the 20,000 ft mark.

This was a technical climb, and we were provided with crampons to attach to our trekking boots. It was a stiff climb through deep snow, and we all walked with some trepidation up the mountain, hoping for mere emotional salvation. As we crossed the threshold and reached the narrow ridge, our senses were overwhelmed with the presence of the August Mountains, seemingly within touching distance. It was nature in its full glory.

We were perched tantalizingly on the narrow ridge; the joy of being in a divine presence overwhelmed all other emotions, including the fear of tumbling down the sliver of a ledge. The presence seeped into our minds and bodies and created an indelible mark, which I can still experience after so many years.

The trek back was an arduous one. We were covering twice the distance that day, partially because it was mostly downhill. The night was falling as we reached our camp for the sleepover. It had been a long 9-hour trek for the day, and our minds and bodies had been pushed. For some, to the breaking point, and they had to be chaperoned back on the mountain mules.

During the trek, my fitness was commented upon by other trekkers, which made me a bit lightheaded, or maybe it was the rarefied air, I ended up announcing my intention to complete the Comrades Marathon. As a display of my readiness, I ran a 10 km trail at around 10,000 feet to stamp my commitment to the challenge.

I have often found that putting a stake in the ground is critical for us to achieve our objectives. It's not about peer pressure or about others judging you in case you fail to achieve your goals; it's more about backing your word and making it count. It helps you eliminate any excuses which may crop up in the way. And you may still fail while trying to achieve your objective, but the critical thing would be that you tried. ***You struggled, and you didn't become an Olympian, but you carried the ethos forward.***

CHAPTER 13

MANAGING FAILURE: MEANDERING IN THE FOREST

While the race sounds daunting, in running between two cities straddled with hills, the training is its more gruelling aspect. A typical week requires 50 km of running, and eventually, you start clocking distances of over 130 km during a week. But it's not about merely clocking mileage. There is a fair amount of thought given to the type of run and to the sequencing of it. Also, the type of terrain you are running on. In case of a hilly run, you need to practice running up and downhill. Both have their challenges. While intuitively, one feels that running uphill will be tougher, and yes, it is quite tough; running downhill is no cakewalk either.

You end up putting a tremendous amount of stress on your quadriceps while running down to decelerate your body, which is gaining momentum. On top of it, the lungs and muscles soon slow down in keeping pace. They struggle to catch up with the pull of gravity and the only thing stopping you from toppling over is your quads. They end up paying a heavy price. Much more than your calves do while running uphill.

Like many runners, I tried to incorporate existing local runs as part of my training program. One such run was a 56 km run in the trails of the Aravalis. It seemed like the perfect training run for setting myself up to conquer Comrades. The race is held at the close by manger forest, resplendent with wildlife; typically, Neelgai (from the deer family) and the like but also a sprinkling of Jackals, Hyenas and Leopards. The run starts early when it is still dark for the 56 km distance runners. I was equipped with a headlamp but with the undulating terrain, it was a struggle to run with any momentum. There was a handful of us and we navigated the first 5 km mostly as a group given that we had still not been blessed by the sun god. As the first rays of the sun hit the landscape, the field widened out and most of us got into a natural rhythm.

I was mostly in the middle of the pack and felt comfortable with my pace. While I would have been happy with a finish, in the back of mind, I was targeting a sub-6-hour finish. I had completed the Bombay full marathon the previous month with a timing of 4 hours and 10 minutes; a distance of 42 km. I had kept an hour and 50 minutes for the additional 14 km of this race and it seemed logical. That's one thing I have realised, and logic doesn't always hold good, that running long-distance races have many moving parts; it is like a blend of different parts with different pieces, woven together with a diligent strategy. Like, from the weather that day to the level of fatigue in the body, to your last good sleep and even what you ate before coming for the race. This reminds me a lot about my corporate life.

A seemingly good conversation with the CEO on the annual business plan could go down the drain if he had an unsavoury interaction with the board member in the morning. Or something as insignificant as the time of the day for the interaction also matters a lot. I realised in one of my assignments, the best time to meet my boss was in the 2nd half of the day. By that time, he had expended most of his energy and hence, I wasn't choked up with work, which also may not be relevant from a long-term perspective. This also ensured that I wasn't quick to react and had enough priming by that time to respond and not merely react.

I reached the first pitstop at the 14 km mark. The turnaround was at a very picturesque location, next to the Badkal lake, and one could see a variety of birds in the vicinity. The lake is away from humanity and is nestled next to a grove. The water is full of varying aquatic creatures as also the winged ones. You can hear the song of the Cranes as also that of Bulbul. This was a mini wildlife reserve. After a round of refreshments, I was headed back to the starting point. The climb from the 18th km mark was a vertical climb, and I felt like running up the aircraft stairs, except that the length was half a km. I managed to run part of the rise and then walked the remaining way up. My ego was somewhat bruised, but it was a small setback given the objective at hand.

I ran back to the finish point and crossed the 28 km mark, again for the 2nd loop. My stamina seemed in fine fettle. I had slowed down a bit; I attributed it to the undulating terrain. By the 30 km mark, there was a visible slowdown in my pace. I was apprehensive about what lay ahead; and by the time I had crossed the 35 km mark, I was sure something was seriously wrong. I had devolved into the walk and run routine. I tried to get some energy back by continuing this pace for the next 3 km. But by the time I had crossed 38 km, I was fully done. Done for the day.

There was a temple nearby with a shade area adjacent to it. I walked my way upto the tree and then sprawled on the ground to get some of the life juices back. My first step in conquering Comrades had been bitten to the dust. My mind had stopped working. I could barely visualise my last month's marathon finish at that point. And here I was, hitting the wall at the 38 km mark. I couldn't find the energy to even think about finishing the run.

This would be my first DNF (did not finish) and it was going to be stuck with me as long as I would be a runner. At that instance, the failure of the run overwhelmed all my past athletic achievements. All I could think was that I had started on the Journey to conquer Comrades and I couldn't even finish my first Ultra Marathon of 56 km. I was devastated.

As I was sinking into my gloom, I saw one of the event organisers driving towards me. Sheepishly, I got into the jeep and could sense his unspoken question: 'What Happened?'

I didn't volunteer any information because I was struggling for answers myself.

I wallowed the whole of that week, drinking from the cup of failure. Trying to come to terms with the dramatic fall in my performance. The usual reasons came to mind: lack of hydration, nutrition and body fatigue, reasonable rest, etc. But nothing could really justify in my mind the abject failure I had experienced that day. Sometimes, no matter how hard you try you are not able to get your answers. In such times you need to wipe the slate clean and restart your journey. And reset, I did.

The intense rigmarole of long runs started again. I was not going to let one setback push aside my objective. The weeks rolled by and I regained some of my confidence. I was going to test myself once again. A good 30 days had elapsed since the last debacle. I had to test my endurance once again. This time I decided to do a series of long runs over a weekend. The objective was to complete 4 runs, both days, in the morning and evening, and cover a distance of 70 km. In some ways, this was tougher than my 56 km trail aspiration. As I had to be mentally fit for each of the runs. Had to have enough motivation to lace up my shoes and get going, rather say, running! I started with 30 km on Saturday morning. Culminating the day with a 10 km run in the evening. I was training with a friend I had made on the journey to Comrades. She ran with me the 30 in the morning and we had decided to do a 21 km run the next day. Nice and early the next day, we started together from our starting point and covered a steady 21 km.

I had covered 61 km that weekend. Close to my objective of 70. I reached home tired and after a sumptuous breakfast, had a nap during the day. The evening was unusually warm, but I didn't want to let go of the objective. I headed for the gym and got onto the treadmill. What started as a 9 km run eventually ended up being a 15 km run on the treadmill. I had crossed my milestone by 6 odd km. I celebrated that day, fully recovered from my self-inflicted rebuke for the failed trail run. But I still needed to cross one more barrier before I could stamp my self-approval of readiness for the "Comrades".

CHAPTER 14

RUNNING IN THE HIMALAYAS & SKINNER'S HORSE

As a part of the Comrades Training, one needs to do a 60-65 km run around 6 weeks prior to the D-Day. As in preparing for the Marathon, the full distance of the Comrades is not run prior to the race. Even the professionals keep their longest run at 70 km. Ideally, on hilly terrain. While we had the Aravalis next door, they were no match for the Lofty Drakensberg Mountains in South Africa.

We decided to ramp up our training program, and my running partner for Comrades and I decided to do the long run in the scenic lap of the Himalayas. The deciding factor was the hilly terrain and potentially colder climes than the Blistering hot hills of Gurgaon. Another of our friends volunteered to pace us for the run. The starting point of the race was the Town of Dehradun, leading to a climb up to Mussoorie and back.

We would be running from an altitude of 450 meters to 2000 meters and back to 450. The elevation of 1500 meters would be traversed in approx. 30 km. It was a stiffer climb than Comrades, albeit a shorter one; but we wanted to go prepared. The run was scheduled for Sunday, early morning.

My friend was gracious enough to bring along her SUV and a driver to take us to Dehradun on Saturday. The initial plan was to reach there Saturday evening, run on Sunday and then head back home on Monday Morning. Allowing our minds and bodies to get some rest. But plans change, and we were to drive back on Sunday evening itself as her son wasn't keeping well.

It was a fine balancing act between passion and family. Too often we feel the tug from various sources, including our professions, but it's always a matter of prioritization and balancing. Somewhere in between, we end up being better time managers and decisive decision-makers. Life's pulls and pushes can either burden us or can help us evolve. It doesn't come easy. Too often it's about bringing balance to our ever-wandering minds. While we may be traversing the length and breadth of the country on our legs, our minds must be firmly rooted. Running is not merely a physical activity, but as I coined it, it's "Meditation in Motion".

We reached our Hotel around 9 pm and after a quick dinner, we hit our beds by 11 pm… We were hoping to start the run by 5:30 am, as getting 6 hours of sleep was essential. Bright and early the next day, we were all set to run up the hills of Mussoorie. It was to be a revelation to me as I had never been to the Queen of the Hill stations. The abode of the iconic author, Ruskin Bond. Many an evening has been spent cavorting with his books. The visualisation of Mussoorie was imprinted on my mind, courtesy the vividness of his descriptions.

At the slotted time, we got down to business. Started at a comfortable pace and soon enough, we hit the inclines, navigating the first 5 km with relative ease. Though, it was a continuous incline albeit of a lower gradient. Post 5 km, the slopes became steeper, pushing our lungs and legs. This wasn't a hill, these were the mighty Himalayas, and they were throwing a challenge at us.

Initially, we were a bit overwhelmed by adversity, but we were long-distance runners and more importantly, fighters. We had driven for 300 km to make this run count. And we were to ensure we get it done to the last mile. The struggle persisted for some more time, and we found our groove not much later interspersing our runs with walks for steep inclines. Soon enough the breath became a bit easier, the tightness of the calves settled down and we were into a slow rhythmic run up the mountain. We had adapted our running gait to the terrain of the mountains and were running with a bit of a forward incline of the body.

There was a fair amount of traffic on the road to Mussoorie. Many weekend picnic-goers were riding to the higher climes for an afternoon well spent. We were being overtaken by a lot of two-wheeler riders, giving us flabbergasted looks. Soon we heard the rhythmic cadence of a troop of soldiers passing us, with one soldier sporting a smirk. I bet he was thinking that 'these middle-aged guys have bitten off more than they can chew.' I was tempted to ramp up my pace, but sanity prevailed. I did not know his destination or the path he had chosen for the same, whereas I knew I was barely 10 km into my run. I had a different path to take and a different mission to accomplish.

Too often in life, we get distracted by what's happening around us and we forget our paths. The paths are chosen by us. Chosen, based on our resources, our dreams, and the canvas provided by destiny. Each one of us is painting a different picture, and what might look rosy to us, might feel thorny to the one holding it. Self-discovery and self-belief are fundamental to our personal growth and development. They form the pillars to our personalities and provide us with the key to unlock our very "own" future.

Our future was limited to the next 40 km. Soon enough, we reached the halfway point, out of breath but full of josh. The tough part of the run was over or so we thought. The climb was done. We had gained 1500 metres over the 30 km of running. It was a new high for us. The road had been full of surprises and one such surprise was when we crossed a Bungalow marked Skinner's Horse.

Having spent some time at the National Defence Academy, besides the fact that my father had donned the uniform for 38 years, the military historian in me relished the thought of being in the front of the residence of Colonel James Skinner, who raised the cavalry regiment, now part of the Indian Army. It felt like being a part of history. A sense of time travel prevailed. The past seemed 'Live'. I could imagine myself riding astride a black steed roaring into battle. Although given our preference for using the legs, we would fit in the role of infantrymen much better.

It reminds me of the time when I met a cavalry officer of the Indian Army in a social gathering. He was into Polo big time and was telling me how long he could continue riding the horse, and also asked me if I was into Horses. I quipped, "I have become a horse myself, given the mileage I am tracking." There were guffaws all around, while I was merely honest. I went on to narrate the story of the annual event organised in Wales every year, *The Man Vs Horse Marathon*.

This is an annual race encovering over 35 km, where runners compete against riders on horseback. The race — which is of a shorter distance than an official marathon road race — takes place in the Welsh town of Llanwrtyd Wells every June. The event started in 1980, when the local landlord, Gordon Green overheard a discussion between two men in a pub, the Neuadd Arms. One man suggested that over a significant distance across the country, man's endurance was equal to that of any horse. Green decided that the challenge should be tested in full public view and organised the first event. In 2004, the 25th race was won by Huw Lobb in 2 hours, 5 minutes and 19 seconds. It was the first time that a man racing on foot had won the race, thereby winning the prize fund of £25,000, which had been growing by £1,000 each year from the race's inception until claimed by a winning runner. The year's race also saw the highest ever number of competitors; 500 runners and 40 horses. The feat was repeated in 2007, when human competitors outpaced the leading equine competitor by around 11 minutes.

There are other Man versus Horse races in Scotland, based in Dores, near Loch Ness; Central North Island, New Zealand and in Prescott, Arizona. I was the talking point for the rest of the party, with my legs being the cynosure of all female eyes.

After the customary selfie with the skinner's Bungalow in the backdrop; I was never able to comprehend before, why people love clicking their snaps; and a new round of Josh, we headed back to Dehradun, still on our legs.

It was mid-afternoon by now, and the sun was at its Zenith. Despite the higher altitude, the temperature was not pleasing at all. Our faces had turned a crimson red, amply hydrated by the sweat pouring down our faces. Every now and then we had to wipe it off, as the salty sweat stung our eyes. We were dousing ourselves with cold water at regular intervals. This brought about temporary relief until the next nutrition stop, wherein the process was replicated. We were like a car from the 1970s which needed to be topped with water in the radiator; else it would heat up and break down.

We were pushing our bodies to the limits. The Brain can be a hard taskmaster. And, even tougher one is our will. It wouldn't stand down till the objective is achieved. Runners can be a bit stubborn like that. ***So can be Leaders with a clear Vision and self-belief***.

We continued our downward run, surprised at how hard it was on our quadriceps. The difficult part was not about maintaining speed but about putting the brakes on. The brakes aka the quadriceps were taking a heavy toll. But we had signed up for this.

We kept striding forth one step at a time and soon enough our starting point was sighted. The spirits soared as did the pace. However, when we were approximately 500 m from the point, having checked our GPS watches, we realised we had covered 58.5 km. It meant going 500 m further than our start point and coming back. This sometimes happens in the long runs. At that moment, that last 1 km seemed like 10 to us, but when you plan to cover 60 km, you do precisely that and by pulling ourselves once again, the last km was put in the bag. The run was through. Our sweat glistened faces did nothing to hide the sense of satisfaction and the wide grins on our faces. As far as we were concerned, Comrades was ours to take.

The day of the race was 40 days away. While we would not be doing such long runs, the training volume would stay high for the next 4 weeks. With a mileage of 90- 100 km per week. Last two weeks, we were to taper the training volumes and intensity. While the body was in fine fettle, it needed to get itself rid of fatigue and any niggles to be charged up for the gruelling task of Comrades.

Organisations are like the human body. They respond to inputs, grow as you nurture them, take up challenges based on the requirement but also need rest and recovery. I have seen too many leaders, whether mid-management or senior, driving their teams to exhaustion and expecting results to change. What it merely does is create a vicious cycle and a lower normal. Effort does not go into thinking about what needs to be done or what can be done but rather, what must be achieved. Teams and Organisations need to be cognizant of people and system fatigue. A fatigued organisation is a recipe for failure. Typically resulting in reduced employee morale and resultant attrition.

CHAPTER 15

THE COUNTDOWN TO PIETERMARITZBURG

We were advancing towards our departure date with rarely a moment not being focused on the run ahead. Last minute checks were done on the preparation for the trip to distant South Africa. Stay arrangements had to be rechecked, airline tickets in place, the expectant waiting for the Visa to come.

As luck would have it, I was due for an office meeting in Singapore and had given my passport with the belief that it would be back stamped with the South African Visa prior to my Singapore trip. Two days before my trip, I had to take matters into my own hands and fly down to Bombay to get the South African consulate to give me back my passport stamped or not. I headed straight to the consulate and camped for the most part of the day. It was quite a nightmare. Some of the consulates behave as if they are the sentinels to the gates of Heaven and do not care about processing things faster; even information flow needs to be curtailed. After making umpteen calls to various entities through official and other means, I was finally able to wrangle my passport back, pleasantly surprised that I had got the visa for South Africa. My training wouldn't go to waste, at last. What a relief it was! Hundreds of hours committed to the challenge of a lifetime will not come to naught. All through the flight to Singapore, I had a constant silly grin on my face, content with the knowledge of having been given the chance to wield the gauntlet.

I was exhausted when I landed in Singapore, having got a short nap on the overnight flight. The running around the Consulate hadn't helped matters. To make matters worse, surprisingly, the immigration queue was a bit too long for comfort and I was somnambulating till the time the immigration officer asked for my visa. Thankfully this was duly authorised, and I was carrying a copy of the same. The same crowd had moved to the taxi area and I had to further dig into my reserves. Lack of sleep can have a debilitating effect on the body. More was in store, as I was expected to be in the office in the next hour. My CEO seemed oblivious to my journey and the time zones. I trudged through the day and fell into the bed without a care in the world, as soon as I reached my hotel room. Old habits die hard, and I was up nice and early for my mid-week run. A meeting in a different country does not need to distort the track of your training even a bit.

Running in Singapore is a feast for the eyes. It's a city with an amalgamation of the Uber Modern with the colonial past. You end up viewing the best of both worlds standing next to each other. As I crossed the Fullerton hotel, I had a breath-taking view of the Marina Bay Sands. Two iconic buildings epitomising Singapore in the best possible way. As I wound my way across the bay, I felt energised with the pulsating energy all around. The Central Business District was vacant barring runners like me. And I have found running ends up creating connections, even amongst strangers, like nothing else I have experienced. A mere nod, a smile, maybe just catching the eye of the fellow runner and the link gets established. It transcends age, gender and race like nothing else does.

Over the next 3 days, I discovered more of Singapore running around, than I had got a chance before in a Taxi. A customary visit to Little India was mandated, as I needed a taste of Indian cuisine. My taste buds were yearning for some spices and they got the due at Saravana Bhavan. My port of call across countries for gorging on South Indian cuisine. I had started my carb-loading, now that the race was just a week to go. I would have barely got 3 days in India before I was to embark for South Africa. The all-important Birthday of my Younger son was to be celebrated. Little did I know of his emotional attachment to my upcoming race. Thankfully, he had stopped asking me whether I would win the race. While I could shirk away from his enthusiasm, I could not easily let go of his expectations from me to complete the race. He wasn't asking for much. Or, so he thought.

The last two days prior to my departure were focused on making his birthday a grand success. Invitations were followed up by personal invites, ensuring appropriate attendance for the grand bash. As in all of his Birthdays, the cake had to be on the theme of a Superhero, that year it was Spiderman. His fascination for superheroes didn't end up merely on the celluloid. I was carrying some of the rub off expectations. Unlike my elder son, who had progressed to seeing me as a father and a human being, I still roved the superhero world as far as the younger one was concerned. I wanted a gradual decline into the world of the living from my superhuman stature and not an abrupt fall.

The party was a grand success, tinged with the emotional plea from my younger son and a confidence-boosting farewell from the elder one. I headed for the airport, with a bit of nerves but a whole lot of emotional baggage. I would have had to cast it aside as soon as I landed on the shores of the African continent.

I was headed across the ocean to a new continent, traversing a distance of 8000 km to reach the starting point of a race merely 90 km in length. Seemed odd. But it wasn't merely 90 km, it was the culmination of a 1200 km journey ending hopefully in a crescendo in the Kingsmead stadium, the arena for many a cricket encounter between India and South Africa. Unlike the cricketing encounter, I was not to be competing with the South Africans but rather matching them step for step. As per estimates, the total steps one takes to finish the Comrades Marathon is 120000. In our daily routines, we end up doing 5000 odd steps. This was 24 days' worth of steps compressed over a 12-hour window with Hills sprinkled generously across the route.

*The Route in itself has 5 key Peaks on the way. Called the BIG 5. Cowies Hill, Fields Hill, Botha's Hill, Inchanga and Polly Shortts. Three of the "***Big Five***" are found in the first half of the race. I can tell you from personal experience, there is nothing "short" about "Polly". And Inchanga is exactly as it sounds, fearsome.*

The field had some 20000 runners from all over the world. It was, after all, the largest and oldest Ultramarathon in the world, 'the Ultimate Human Race.'

CHAPTER 16

LOSING FAITH

The Bus visit

As a part of acclimatising the participants to the history of the marathon and also the race, a Bus tour is conducted. It is usually guided by one of the veteran runners who takes questions from the participants and in a few cases, asks some of his own. Our guide was a robust-looking man in his sixties and seemed a bit of a Martinet. As we were going along the route, my anxiety levels started climbing, because the distance and the terrain were sinking in. And my confidence was walking a tight trapeze.

The first port of call was the Comrades Museum at Pietermaritzburg.

It's an old restored Victorian house, with as much character as the grand race it depicts and holds the history and memorabilia of the Ultimate human race. Comrades Marathon House serves as the headquarters for the Comrades Marathon and a museum to the history of the race and its victors. It has an accurate to scale (1:25000) model of the race route. The 'big five' hills on the up route challenge appear in the order of Cowies Hill, Fields Hill, Botha's Hill, Inchanga, and then, Poly Shorts. The strenuous downhill distance also tackles some climbing faces including the hillsides of Inchanga, Alverstone, Cowies Hill, and Botha's Hill. Historical museum photographs document the beginning of this global gathering initiated in 1921 by World War 1 veteran, Vic Clapham.

Perusing the spoils of the victor and the records they had created put most of us in awe of what we were trying to achieve. The museum also depicts how the field expanded and allowed blacks and women to participate from 1975 onwards. Sports had been an equaliser much before Apartheid was abolished between the years 1990-1994. After some customary clicks at the altar of the running gods, we boarded our buses back to Durban.

As we chatted along, our guide asked us if any of us had done 2500 km of training over the past 6 months. I thought he was pulling our leg. To my utter surprise, a couple of hands were raised. An American lady had trained for 3000 km. I was about to fall off my seat. As this polling continued, I realised I was amongst the handful of people still to record their training mileage. Finally, when he asked for distances from 1000-1200 km, I raised my hand.

"Guys, you have done the bare minimum required for completing the race."

With these words, he stamped his approval onto me. A sense of relief seeped in as I rejoiced at having crossed the 1000 km mark. Albeit not by much.

The rest of the journey was a bit of a haze, I kept vacillating between confidence and anxiety. Having sensed my swinging emotions, the runner next to me tried to chat me up. John was from England and had recently recovered from a Hip fracture while gallivanting with his girlfriend in New Zealand on a bike. I asked him how it had impacted his running, to which he quipped, "Mate, my timing has worsened. I am doing the full marathon in 3 hours and 20 minutes nowadays."

I took a hard swallow as my personal best without having been involved in any bike accident with either girlfriend or wife, was a slow 3 hours and 50 minutes. To top it all, he looked much older than me (I was 40 at that time). I couldn't hold back my curiosity and finally asked him about his age.

John reverted, "I will be turning 60 this year."

This acclimating bus ride was taking a heavy toll on my self-confidence. I realised that if I stayed on this bus long enough, then my chances of finishing Comrades would vaporise.

I practically scrambled off the bus walking back to the seafront property I was staying in, in a daze. The cool breeze and the sound of the lapping waves did little to raise my spirits. I assigned the responsibility of rejuvenating my senses to the cool beer down my throat. The bubbly drink achieved what nature was found wanting at.

Well, each situation requires a different solution. Answers and solutions always are contextual, and the key is to understand the prevalent environment for an optimum solution. As a leader, I have often found that sometimes a mere acknowledgment of your team member's contribution or situation or the effort put in does more than any other gratification. A salary hike in itself will not change the employee engagement if the working conditions are repressive. I have seen cofounders and senior employees of a bank let go of their ESOPs merely because the environment was too toxic to be offset by money alone. At one instance, by the time a bank had eventually gone public, not one member of the original team was present barring the CEO and Founder. It seemed even the wealth which was created had serious legality concerns. Leaders need to remember that the most lasting legacy they leave behind is not merely the Business results but the camaraderie they have created with their teams. The same lasts much beyond professional engagement and eventually seeps into our personal domain. One of my closest friends and well-wishers is my Ex-Boss. I reported to him for a mere 2 years but have created a life-long bond.

I had landed in Durban just a day before and was already going through anxiety pangs. No matter how much we try to evade it off, the nervousness continues to stay perched on our shoulders and every time we look back, it tends to screech out its presence like a talkative parrot.

The beer had lasted me for the night and had provided a sound sleep, but the next day being new, I was still struggling with my confidence. Merely parroting my training journey was not sufficient for me to walk with confidence without a care in the world. I decided to go for a short run on the beach to loosen my body and solidify my resolve. This time the elements had a better impact. The sound of the waves provided a cadence to my running. The gentle breeze soothed my nerves and the eyes were feasting on the beauty of Mother Nature. The sparkling blue ocean made it look like a giant swimming pool albeit a turbulent one at that. As has happened many times in the past, I stumbled upon a Eureka Moment. I had been carrying the burden of trying to be successful for too long. I had got scared of failing. A perfect recipe for choking. I allowed myself to accept that it was a challenging race and non-completion is not a failure, although it would be disappointing. My urge to be successful was overshadowing my strengths and my training. Acceptance of the possibility of not finishing the race released me from my self-inflicted mental cage. I was liberated. Reflecting in my ear to ear grin while running at a fast pace to the bewilderment of the onlookers, wondering what secret I had unveiled to display such euphoria.

Often in our work, we end up focusing on the possibility of failing so much that the opportunity to be successful recedes to a corner. Too often this is a result of the culture defined by organisation, in which the repercussion for failure is much higher than the reward for success. Finding a balance between trying new things and failing and repeating the same mistakes is what organisations need to strive for. Leaders need to foster this approach. This is not necessarily reflected in documented policies, but more importantly, is reflected in day to day engagements. While heading distribution for a Life Insurance company, I realised the impact of my communication, when it was being cascaded to approx. 3000 FTEs and 2000 contractual employees. My email was not merely a communication for the next course of action but was also a subtle reminder of the ethos and values of the company.

I have made many presentations to small groups of potential investors and board members or a big group like in a company town hall or a Ted talk, and every time I felt a sense of uneasiness putting across my thoughts. I kept reminding myself, what I am presenting is not merely the work of the past week but a culmination of learning in more than a decade. We need to remind ourselves what all has been done to reach the place we are now as a stepping stone to greatness. And we arrive here with our grit, perseverance, and hard work.

Back at the hotel, I pounced on the big breakfast spread. I had enough and more excuses to indulge in Gluttony. As a precursor to the race day, I was to enhance my carbohydrates intake so that the muscles store enough of them to fuel the race. Over the years of my running adventures, I have interacted with thousands of runners, some have become friends for life and not surprisingly, a good proportion belongs to the corporate world handling senior assignments; I also found a common thread, besides the zest for life– a soft corner for food and beer. Unlike what many may assume, runners are no way ascetic in their lives; instead, they use running and other endurance sports to balance their extravagances.

There were 5 of us from Gurgaon for the big race and we had been friends for some time now. After enjoying a feast with the other Indian runners, we headed for the expo. The one place where all of us would converge before the race, besides doing the administrative stuff of completing our registrations and picking up our bibs and goody bags: to basically soak in the energy of our fellow runners hailing from 80 countries. It was kind of an informal Sporting United Nations happening on the tip of the African continent. The Expo is a grand affair. In my rather short running journey, I had never encountered an expo of this grandeur. Besides the official stalls, there was a plethora of sporting brands dispensing wares unknown to most of us. We were like children in a candy store. Enticed by apparel and running accoutrements. We had to work hard on ensuring that our wallets remained viable for the remaining part of the trip.

One gets surprised by the varying nationalities and backgrounds, including the age brackets. The oldest finisher of the comrades' Marathon was an 80-year-old and left half the finishers behind him in the quest for writing history. The most prominent teachers for me in my life have been new and varied experiences. This was one such experience. Seeing someone break the barriers of age so profoundly was an eye-opener.

CHAPTER 17

THE CHARGE OF THE LIGHT BRIGADE

"Half a league, half a league,

Half a league onward,

All in the valley of Death

Rode the six hundred.

Forward, the Light Brigade!"

- The Charge of the Light Brigade

By Alfred Lord Tennyson

The next two days were over in a jiffy. We were mostly connecting with runners across the world, sharing experiences and a few laughs. There was a run organised for the international runners on a penultimate day from the race day. It was an informal gathering of non-native runners. For us to get our nervous energies out and to know each other and maybe, learning something new. The run culminated at the Hilton, followed by a round of beer and a pep talk by Bruce Fordyce. He is a South African marathon and an Ultramarathon athlete. He is known for having won the South African Comrades Marathon for a record of nine times, of which eight wins were consecutive. He also won the London to Brighton Ultramarathon three years in a row. His presence was awe-inspiring and it took some time for us to listen to him over our fuzzy heads. We concluded the day with a vote of confidence from the legend himself and felt more confident of achieving success.

The night before the run was a tense affair. The race was to start at precisely 5:30 am. I needed to be at the starting point no later than 5 am. The starting point was at Pietermaritzburg, while we were staying at Durban as the race would conclude here. We were to board the buses at 3:30 in the morning, to arrive at the starting point at 5. Which meant getting up at 2 am and leaving for the Bus pickup location at 3 am. It was all a bit too early even for my taste. I was tucked into bed promptly at 7 pm, hoping to catch 7 hours of sleep; but with butterflies doing the tango, I eventually fell asleep around 10 pm. I barely got 4 hours of sleep.

The hotel was buzzing with activity. They had been kind enough to prepare a special breakfast for us. In the week of Comrades, these towns get transformed. The overwhelming number of runners and their supporters create a carnival-like atmosphere. Our hotel primarily had runners, some from South Africa, others from as far as England and Brazil. In the morning, the euphoria was significantly subdued... we exchanged barely discernible nods. I wasn't the only one having nerves. It felt as if all of us were headed for a battle; while we would be fighting together, our personal journeys would still be "ours" only. And how many of us would emerge unscathed.

The owner of the hotel was kind enough to drop us at the starting point. The spirit of camaraderie was palpable everywhere. As soon as boarding completed, we headed for Pietermaritzburg via the highway. While running back to Durban, we had to take a longer route through the countryside. The journey passed away in a blur. Some of us were lucky enough to catch 40 winks on the drive to Pietermaritzburg.

At sharp 5 am, we disembarked from the buses trying to find our pens. Based on our marathon timings we were allocated slots. An Army would be running that route. A total of 20,000 runners would be running that day, hoping to culminate their gruelling training, to conquer the coveted Comrades medal. The atmosphere was electrifying. It was still dark. The South African winters had started. It was bitterly cold.

There had been instances when the temperature touched the freezing point. We were to start cold and finish the run at the coast, where it was typically in the 30s. The weather change was dramatic. Because of the weather variations, one had to dress up in layers and had to keep discarding them as the sun rose and the body started heating up by the extensive running. But the cold could do nothing to subdue the electrifying energy of the event.

Music was playing in the background and raising our spirits even higher. We were drawing energy from each other and itching to start the race. Each one felt like a star in the spotlight albeit in a sea of humanity. There is a special Zulu song which is played every year before the start of the race; *Shosholoza*; the essence of the song being to go forward to the mountains.

Which we were about to. The song has a haunting note to it that makes one's hair stand on edge. The song is followed by the famous song, "Chariots of Fire", the default theme of the Olympic Games, immortalized by the iconic movie of the same name, featuring runners.

The emotions were rising to a crescendo. We were all expectant now. Soon enough the countdown began. Tradition demands that the run starts with the crowing of a Rooster, which is actually a mimicry. And so, it did, twice, post which the cannon was blasted, and the race began. We were off or at least, the ones in the front rows were. It may take anywhere from 5 to 10 minutes to reach the starting point depending on your seeding. Unlike other races, one's time didn't start when he or she crossed the start line, but rather when the cannon was fired. In running parlance, it is a gun-to-gun race. This meant one had that much less time to finish the race because at sharp 5:30 pm, 12 hours hence, the finish line would be blocked and one may have completed the distance, but not the race. While this may seem apocryphal, I had seen a video in which a runner was blocked from finishing the race, because he had exceeded the time limit by a second.

This seemed unfair but when you look at various aspects of life, from an overall view, you realise that not all of us start our journeys from the same point. We may have some advantages and some disadvantages but in the end, if we have it in us to complete something, nothing can stop us. We can't spend our lifetime thinking of our disadvantages and must rather focus on what needs to be achieved. It's a lifelong learning for me.

Focus on "Doing".

The race was truly ON now. I crossed the starting line after about 5 minutes. It was still quite cold and dark. I was carefully treading my way, avoiding the cat's-eye on the road, and also ensuring I wasn't stepping on anyone's shoes while equally being mindful of my own shoes. Didn't want to end the race for anyone just as soon as it had begun; hoping others would also be kind enough with me. There had been instances of runners losing one of their shoes and in the stream of runners following behind, they were unable to trace their shoes. I cannot imagine the anguish and pain they must have felt. The sense of utter frustration. Anyway, to happy thoughts now, I was maintaining a steady pace and was in no hurry to overtake anyone; there was also no room for much manoeuvring. The route was hilly from the word go and just as we were finishing our 2nd kilometre, we encountered one such nameless hill. While the run is famous for the "Big 5", there were numerous unnamed hills along the route. Sometimes it's good to not know the count of such hills. I completed the first one and was a bit out of breath. Took a walking break. The thing about Comrades is, in the total 90 km distance you are likely to walk 15-20 km. Only the top 10 finishers run the full course. The gradient and the length of some of these hills make it perilous to run up, also in terms of creating fatigue in one's system too early in the race. Since there was no hurry to finish, there was none to run up the hills.

You have to be pragmatic and swallow your pride. There were smiles all around. Now that we had commenced our expedition, the tension had melted away. I was amazed at the crowd support for the first 7 odd km or so. People had lined up next to the road and cheering the runners. My experience of supportive crowds was epitomised in Bombay but I was slowly getting a sense of the grandeur of this race and was keenly awaiting the plethora of experiences I would encounter.

I was beginning to feel a bit warm in my multi-layered clothing, which I was planning to hand over to the less fortunate onlookers. But I couldn't have been too hasty about it, as the temperature could vary quite a bit. Soon enough we crossed over Polly shorts, which is a killer on the way up in the alternating sequence of the Comrades run. By the time we hit the bottom of Polly shorts, the temperature had also dipped. I was thankful for having researched when to discard extra layers and such. As we "marched on", the confidence levels began to stabilize. No more was I encountering a to and fro of emotional imbalance.

The one thing about Comrades is that unlike other runs, which tell you how much distance has been covered; the markers for Comrades tell you the distance to be covered. So, after 15 km of running, when you encounter a signboard saying 75 km to go, it kind of takes a bit of getting used to.

Every time you believe that the challenge which lies ahead of you is impossible, you just need to glance back over your shoulder and see what all you have accomplished. Magnification of problems is a mental thing and so is the miniaturizing of it. I could be concerned with 75 km more running to be done or be confident in the 1200 km of running I had done to reach that place. It's all in mind. Focus on the journey and not the destination.

We indeed reached into rural South Africa, and the supporters had thinned out. Though there were still dispersed supporters on the way, their enthusiasm was infectious. Kids were sitting on their fathers' shoulders, a couple cheering us with placards; a small child was running across to hand over candies. It was truly remarkable. It kept the mental energy right at the top, and the energy drinks and gels were doing the same for the body. I had shed my layers and my nervousness completely.

CHAPTER 18

BAMBOO TREE

One will hear this term often in running, “Dig Deep.” Just about every coach exhorts runners to “dig deep.” Digging deep not only means working hard but working your hardest. It means completing workouts no matter how tired you may feel. It means reaching into your heart and finding the will to try to get to the next level of excellence.

This also happens in practice runs. Especially the longer kind. The human mind can only push the body so much before the mind starts getting distress signals to stop the torture the body is going through. This is a natural response and more often than not should be heard. But when you are breaking barriers, the need to be deaf becomes paramount. Deaf to the voice and to the pain. This is when the inner voice shouts out to the mind, to dig deep into the reserves. When we dig, we are basically finding the deep roots of stamina which have been embedded over time.

This brings me to an interesting story of the Bamboo tree.

Like any plant, growth of the Chinese Bamboo Tree requires the basic element of water, fertile soil, sunshine. In its first year, there are no visible signs of activity. In the second year, again, no growth can be seen above the soil. The earth is bald like Shetty's pate. The third and the fourth year come and go, and yet no signs of any life above the ground or sub-terranean. It seems as if all the effort is going to waste.

The patience starts getting tested and we begin to wonder if our efforts (caring, water, etc.) will ever be rewarded. This becomes especially pertinent in the "Now" times. Immediate gratification vs nurtured patience. The need to accomplish now and reap the rewards has been a social construct which has created a stronghold in our current society.

Finally, after 4 years of sustenance being provided, in the fifth year–a miracle unfolds. The Bamboo tree grows. And does it grow? It propels itself to lofty heights, dwarfing even the tallest of trees. The Chinese Bamboo Tree grows 80 feet in just six weeks! This is data and not perception.

This phenomenal growth begets many questions.

Does the Chinese Bamboo Tree really grow 80 feet in six weeks?

Was it merely the case of the tree lying dormant for four, only to grow exponentially in the fifth?

Or is there something more than what meets the eye. Is there another plausible explanation?

By any chance, was the tree growing underground, developing a root system strong enough to support its potential for outward growth in the fifth year and beyond?

The answer seems obvious. It was making its foundations strong for the exponential growth to be supported.

Had the tree not developed a strong unseen foundation, it could not have sustained its life as it grew and thrived in all its glory. The same principle is true for Leaders. Leaders, who patiently toil towards worthwhile dreams and goals, building strong character while overcoming adversity and challenge, grow the strong internal foundation to handle success. They create the organisation robustness for exponential growth.

Had the farmer who had sown the seed with much hope, dug up his little seed every year to see if it was growing, he would have stunted the Chinese Bamboo tree's growth as surely as a caterpillar is doomed to a life on the ground if it is freed from its struggle inside a cocoon prematurely. The struggle in the cocoon is what gives the future butterfly the wing power to fly, just as tension in muscles as we exercise strengthen our muscles, while muscles left alone will soon atrophy.

The Chinese Bamboo Tree is a perfect allegory to our own experience with personal growth and change (whether we are working on ourselves or coaching others). It is never easy. It's slow to show any progress. It's frustrating and unrewarding at times.

New skills are developed as a consequence of this struggle. Like the caterpillar, we can unfold our true glory only through struggle, strengthening our core and developing untold aspects.

What can we learn from the Bamboo Tree?

Can we stay focused and continue to believe in what we are doing even when we don't see immediate results? In a culture driven by instant gratification–this is our biggest challenge.

When runners are trying to dig in deep, it is not merely the will power which allows him or her to propel forward. Years have gone into creating that extra reserve of energy and strength. Nothing worthwhile comes easy; and if it does, it does not gratify the fulfilment we seek.

So is the case with Path breaking Leaders, they have grown their roots, developed knowledge, skills and fortitude over the years, the manifestation of it is not in the near future but more in the long term.

Their actions were not determined by the prospect of easy or immediate results.

As I pondered these-----------------thoughts, I wondered; have I invested enough in my core, in my roots? Do I have strong and deep roots I can dig into?

The fulfilment of the race will be the validation. All I can do right now is to pick myself up and try to dig deep. Deeper than I ever have.

CHAPTER 19

LEADERS ARE MADE, NOT BORN

We were approaching the first significant climb, not a tough one at that, of Umlas road, the highest point of the route. The rest of the BIG 5 were waiting for us; generally in safaris, we seek out the other BIG 5 (the popular big five game in Africa includes the lion, leopard, rhinoceros elephant, and Cape buffalo).

I saw an exciting pair running together. Mother and son, pacing together with smiles crossing their faces. They were a sight to behold.

Seeing the instance of the perfect bond between the mother and the offspring, my mind wandered to my younger son and his fervent imposition for me to complete the race. Nothing moves us more than our need to keep our image afloat in our children's minds; akin to personalities, we may hero-worship. I recollect the time I had gatecrashed a lecture being given by Late Field Marshal Sam Maneckshaw. He was a personality to behold. And if anything came close to hero-worship for me, it was towards my father and him—both men in the uniform.

With a distinguished military career that spanned over four decades and fighting five major wars, Field Marshal Sam Hormusji Framji Jamshedji Manekshaw or Sam Manekshaw is undoubtedly one of the most celebrated military men in independent India. Starting his service with the British Indian Army during World War II, Sam Bahadur was the first Indian Army Officer to be promoted to the position of a Field Marshal.

He is primarily known for his heroics during the 1971 Indo-Pak War when he was the Chief of Army Staff. Indian Forces successfully initiated operations on the Eastern and Western front, and eventually won the war that led to the creation of Bangladesh under his leadership.

When Indira Gandhi asked Sam Manekshaw if the Indian Army was ready for a war against Pakistan in April 1971, he told her about the inevitable defeat if India attacked East Pakistan untimely.

He was cognizant of the challenges that lay ahead; from Logistics to getting troops ready for warfare in swampy lands, but most importantly, he was aware of the havoc the monsoons would create, making armour irrelevant to the war; potentially making the Indian Army lose its decisive strengths.

He was a man known for his courage and wit, and this was, inarguably, his most famous quote on leadership:

"Give me a man or a woman with common sense and who is not an idiot, and I assure you can make a leader out of him or her. Professional knowledge and professional competence are the main attributes of leadership. Unless you know, and the men you command know that you know your job, you will never be a leader."

Coming from a man who presided over possibly the largest surrender of enemy troops (The Pakistani army of 93,000 surrendered to the Indian Army in the War of Liberation for Bangladesh) in modern history, marginally ahead of the 90,000 soldiers of the German army who surrendered in Stalingrad, it carries tremendous insight and weight.

His words had a lasting impact on me and one thing which stayed with me was his brave approach in **doing the right thing despite staggering odds**.

I have led teams over the past 15 years or so, and have always been cognizant of the positive impact I can have on their value systems and their professions. Many a time, the simple reward has been, by being remembered fondly by such team members long past they had stopped reporting to me. It warms the cockles of the heart.

From then onwards, it was about steady running... running up half the hill and walking the remaining. Trying and getting some speed on the down sloped hills... Each hill was negotiated not in kilometres but was broken down into bends and trees...Walk till the next bend; run till the next tree and so on. Comrades had changed the reference point for us. Milestones were measured in one electricity pole to the next. This was the way of keeping your mind and body aligned. While running such long-distance races, the objective is obvious; that of completing it, the reference points of achievement have to be continuously changed by breaking the whole goal down significantly into manageable chunks. From the 28 km mark right up to 40 km, it was a steady climb barring a small patch called Harrison flats. This was a tough climb. We were continuously gaining elevation and the legs were beginning to feel the strain. We were still short of the halfway mark.

One of the BIG 5s was looming ahead of us, “Inchanga”. As you approach the daunting climb, you cross an alligator farm. In our Bus tour, we were shown the precise location from where the crocodiles had come on to the road a couple of times. I am not sure whether the guide was joking or not. In my current tired state, the mind started playing tricks, and I was cagey as I crossed the stretch of road, which was infested with Jaws. By some luck, the field had spread out significantly, and I was a lonely runner on that short stretch. The mind was doing some quick calculations and wondering if I could outrun an alligator in my current state. Thankfully, I was not tested that day.

After the alligator scare, the climb to Inchanga seemed almost a relief. The mind can play tricks on you; this trick, for a change, benefited me.

The next 4 kilometres which followed were a gentle downhill. I relished each step of the run. It was a break I was looking forward to, but having scouted the route a couple of days back, I knew there were serious challenges ahead. This was when I needed to focus; focus on the now, at that moment.

In the pursuit of the future, we end up compromising our present. In the process, we bring forward our worries. This is the cause of significant stress in personal and professional life. We need to be existentialists in adverse conditions. We have to focus on that tiny sliver of time which we can "own".

Soon I was at the halfway point. At Drummond, another of the "BIG 5" surfaced up within the cut off. I climbed up a ridge to pick flowers and place it at Arthur's seat, and wished him a Good morning; a long-standing tradition to ensure that you have an excellent second half. It's in honour of the first winner of the Comrades Marathon; Arthur Newton. As per legend, he used to take a break at this point and enjoy a pipe before commencing the rest of the gruelling race. I wouldn't mind having one myself, along with a chilled bottle of beer. But that would have to wait because unlike Arthur, I was a mere Amateur in Long distance running. I was cognizant of my then-current capabilities and what was achievable for me at that point in time. I was treading my path, carved by me with sweat, blood, and some tears. I owned my actions...

CHAPTER 20

CHALLENGES & THE ESSENCE OF LIFE

Being well within the cut-off wasn't any consolation because the cut-off timings are generous. Even if you cross these points ahead of the stipulated time, it is not guaranteed that you'd have a timely finish of 12 hours. While it can be disheartening to miss the cut-offs; in the end, it is about lowering your disappointment, I believe, to be disqualified at the 40 km mark rather than at the 80 km mark. There is also a health angle. If you are not in sync with the requisite time cut-offs, then possibly your body is under some undue stress.

For me, I had to change gears, merely the mental kind. Sometimes, you cannot look back and consider what you have achieved but rather what lies in store for you. I had to merely finish a bit more than a marathon and I had 6 and a half hour to do so. Based on the situations, you need to alternate between looking what you have accomplished and what needs to be done. The cat was still not in the bag. Any long-distance runner will tell you that marathons are tough. Professional marathon runners take a week's rest after finishing a marathon. Basically, to heal the muscles. The muscle fibres are torn and frayed in the pounding they receive over the 42.2 km distance. And here were 20000 of us, taking up the gauntlet to run another marathon after having finished one in hilly terrain.

A rather old gentleman was walking next to me, on one of the many hills on the way. His bib mentioned 41; that wasn't his age, it was the number of times he had finished the race. I asked him about what drove him to come year on year and do it.

He replied, "It's the challenge which brings me every year."

It reminded me of what **George Mallory**, the famous mountaineer, had said:

"People ask me, 'What is the use of climbing Mount Everest?' and my answer must at once be, 'It is of no use. There is not the slightest prospect of any gain whatsoever. Oh, we may learn a little about the behaviour of the human body at high altitudes, and possibly medical men may turn our observation to some account for aviation. But otherwise, nothing will come of it. We shall not bring back a single bit of gold or silver, not a gem, nor coal or iron... ***If you cannot understand that there is something in man which responds to the challenge of this mountain and goes out to meet it,***

that the struggle is the struggle of life itself, upward and forever upward, then you won't see why we go.

What we get from this adventure is just sheer joy. And joy is, after all, the end of life. We do not live to eat and make money. We eat and make money to be able to live. That is what life means and what life is for.'"

The joy of completing a challenge is possibly one of the biggest motivating factors for humans to search for newer and tougher boundaries. And unlike material possessions, the joy permeates time and environment. It resides in us. We thrive in challenging situations. Sure, it brings about discomfort but what it also brings alongside are possibilities. An opportunity to expand one's horizons. The growth of the human race may have evolved to ensure the survival of the race, but now it has metamorphosed into a quest for seeking challenges, of exploring new horizons.

The next of the BIG 5 was Botha's hill. I had practically finished 50 km of the race, and the longest of the steep climbs were over. The sharp descent had started for Durban from now on. Barring a few hills, I was to run downhill, albeit not at a comfortable gradient.

It can get steep, and the legs might scream, but the mind plays dumb. Neither listening nor responding.

CHAPTER 21

THE UNEXPECTED: IN LIFE & WORK

I was running with relative ease when somewhere around the 55th km mark, my calf injury rose like the loch ness monster; I was under severe duress, and applied ice and spray liberally. It gave me temporary relief, but there was a distinct hardening and worsening of the calf. I was under severe mental stress. I had to rectify my situation because mere walking would not have achieved the objective. I would have ended up missing the cut off with 35 kilometres still to go. As I limped my way forward, I came across a medical station; runners with various conditions were getting themselves tended to. Finally, I was able to catch the attention of the lady medic, who applied a tightly wound compression bandage around my calf, which made me apprehensive. I wasn't sure if my leg would be mobile enough to run. She reassured me that it would work just fine. True to her words, I could walk and run unrestrained, and the calf was not giving me any more trouble. I felt fighting fit. The Gladiator was ready to continue the duel.

She was my Florence Nightingale.

I had this injury in one of my long weekend runs. It had put a stop to my training for more than a week, and intensive physiotherapy had got me out of it. The lady medic had done wonders for me. There were many like me with Bandages wrapped around their calves or thighs. The incessant pounding and the undulating terrain can be merciless on the body. Typically, about one in three of all runners experience cramps in the run. There have been some fatalities too, 7 participants had died while trying to finish the race. During my run, one of the participants completed the race, only to collapse and be rushed to the hospital. He passed away in the hospital after 2 weeks. His kidney and Liver had shut down. These two organs are the driving force for doing such athletic activities, besides the heart and the Lungs. The liver helps convert energy to propel our bodies forward, whereas the Kidneys help remove toxic waste. If either of the two organs fails, it can be fatal.

As I gathered my bearings back and strode forward, I thought about preparing for the unexpected. Whether in sports or life, something will always spring up which you had least expected to. Too often in my career, I have found corporate presentations to be ***prepared for the unexpected***. I have struggled for years to be ready for my presentation to my seniors, especially my boss, and found to my chagrin that the questions asked are something I had not been prepared for. The reason is that there is emotion involved when I present, which limits my capability to see the situation from multiple perspectives or to see it with complete objectivity.

And which has made me develop something called, ***"What's the headline? And why?"***

CHAPTER 22

GETTING BACK ON THE HORSE: AIMING FOR BRONZE

Winston Park

I was shaken and stirred after my fall. I got my focus re-aligned to the task at hand. 20 km of running was all that was required. There seemed to be enough time at hand. The running route had become a carnival. The route was lined with supporters enjoying their Sunday in the sun. Some picnics were going on. Others were rooting for their favourite runners. Every now and then, I would hear my name called out; and even though it was written across my bib; it felt reassuring to be egged on by them. My handlebar moustache ensured I got more than my share of shout outs, often goaded to twirl it for the audience, which I happily complied with. After all, my energy levels were being fuelled by their support.

The smell of the barbecue was tantalising. As were the offers to down a beer. Both had to be ignored for the greater good. The plethora of Cheerleaders along the way was remarkable. They did raise the spirits of one and all. Not once during the run do you feel alone, from the runners to the enthusiastic supporters, it's all a big family. One such volunteer was a big surprise; it was none other than Shaun Pollock, the South African all-rounder who had made a mark for himself in the cricketing Annals. He offered me some water and although I was fully hydrated, I could hardly even imagine refusing the offer.

I reached the 71st km cut-off, the Cowies Hill in 8:48:53 hours... I thought I had a shot at the Bronze medal. No, I wasn't coming third in the field of 20,000. I was merely a student of primary school with a galaxy of Graduates next to me. Comrades has various categories of medals based on one's finishing time. A 9 hr- 11 hr finish implied a Bronze medal. I was eager to earn the same. I needed to do 18.28 km, almost all of it downhill within 2 hours 11 minutes. I believed I had enough juice in me.

The record for the down run was 5:18:19.

Having done the race, it is still beyond my comprehension to understand such timings.

My knee was not in sync with my plans to achieve the bronze medal. No sooner than I increased my pace on down-hills, I got a shooting pain in my right knee. Two years back, I had been out of action for a knee injury. It brought back some fierce memories. This was right before my first full

Marathon in Bombay. Downhill, I couldn't increase pace because of my knee, and in whichever climbs were left now, I couldn't increase my pace because of my calf. I was in an unenviable position. A couple of friends made during the short stay in Durban egged me on as they crossed me to fulfil their dreams. Running Comrades for the first time.

Sometimes just finishing the race is enough. This was one such day. We encounter tough situations in our life and merely staying the course takes all out of us. Too often, we are unkind to ourselves, failing to realise the effort it took to tide through the tough time. I decided to be kind with myself and focused on finishing the run in the stipulated time of that under 12 hours.

Game plans must align with reality, and the mere imposition of will doesn't get the desired results.

During the run, while navigating one of the umpteen hills, I asked one of the fellow South African runners about his game plan to finish the race. He remarked, "The legs will take me through the 70 km, and the mind till 85." I asked, "What about the remaining distance?"

He replied: *"The crowds will take me through, to the finish."*

Every year there is a theme for the race. This year it was: ***"Hard is what makes it great."***

I had done the hard part or at least most of it. Now, I was waiting for greatness to descend over me.

As we forged ahead, each kilometre seemed a bit more complicated than the last one. No, it was not the mind playing games. The body was being pushed to the limits and beyond. As the pain fest continued, we encountered the last of the "BIG 5". Cowies Hill was the final big climb before the finish line. Although there were still a couple of smaller ones left after that. We walked our way up the hill for most of the part. Pride had been pocketed by then, and we walked up the hill with a grin on our faces. Ratification of the finish would suffice; killing your legs on the last big hill would not earn any brownie points. By this time, the philosophy had evolved to just putting one foot in front of the other. It was mind over matter.

CHAPTER 23

THE ESSENCE OF A LEADER

The suburbs were resplendent with the ethnic Indian Population. The Indian runners were welcomed like long lost friends. Like heroes, back from the battlefront. Well, we might have won many battles that day but the ultimate ones still presented themselves. We were headed for the 45th cutting, or Sherwood.

An exciting history lies behind the origin of Sherwood. It is named after the Sherwood Foresters, a nickname attributed to the 45th Regiment of Foot of the British army, stationed there during the middle of the 19th century. The cutting through the hill, valiantly carried out with pick and shovel for which they were responsible, is still called '45th cutting' today.

The runners were not cutting through the hill with pick and shovel but rather with their legs and endurance. Each one making a mark for themselves. Engraving their names in the history books. Some have taken a step more; there is a wall of fame just before Drummond. It captures the names of the winners and the greats of the run. For a not very large sum of money, you can get your name engraved out there.

As of now, engraving my achievement on my sons' minds and hearts was enough and more.

Soon enough, we entered the city of Durban. Full of hustle-bustle. One side of the roads was earmarked for the runners. The cheering became more intense, and for a moment, I could forget the agony of my body. We started navigating the twists and turns of the road, with a smile slowly appearing on our tired glistening faces.

As I saw the onlookers cheering us on, as if wanting us to finish the race more than we did, I had a Eureka Moment...

"You know you have arrived as a Leader when your ambition to Lead is overshadowed by your team's desire to be led by you."

CHAPTER 24

MY SONS' HERO

The stadium loomed right ahead, reminiscent of the Titanic, creating a lifelong imprint on us. But instead of taking us down, this made us soar in our respective journeys as runners, as individuals and maybe even as Leaders.

The bubbling energy was slowing down, making its way to my legs and lungs. In spite of having run for 88 odd kilometres, the sight of the stadium pumped me up with Adrenaline. I ran fast, possibly the fastest I had done in the whole race. Nothing could stop me from achieving the long-sought goal now. Entering the stadium was a euphoric phenomenon. The stadium was lit up and brimming with Spectators and Supporters. We had to take a loop of the stadium, the most gratifying 400 metres I had ever run in my life. The last 100 metres was a dream finish. Running with all that was left in me with long strides and the arms pumping me into forward propulsion.

I crossed the finish line. I had finished the race. I was a Comrades Finisher.

The volunteers started garlanding me with the Finisher medal. I had been told that most first-time finishers end up crying at the finish line. I was not one of them or was I?

Throughout the run, I had kept my phone switched off, unsure of the battery surviving the 12-hour journey. The instance I switched it on, it came to life with a loud ring from my wife. She was Euphoric and wanted to hear all about the race, and I choked. Words failed me. I couldn't talk, and my eyes were moist. The plethora of emotions which engulfed was too much to comprehend. I could barely speak anything.

"Tell Aryaman & Shaurya, Dad finished the race."

With that, I came down on my knees and put the months of the burden off my shoulders. It had been a heavy responsibility but it was every bit worth it.

Up to then, for me, it was about putting a tick mark across the goal. And now, I had done it.

What Next?

Onto the "Up run" next year...For one more journey of a lifetime...

EPILOGUE

As promised to myself, after getting my bearings in pace, I headed for the International Runners tent, to guzzle down my first cold beer in a long time. It felt like nectar going down my throat. I didn't have much of a desire for food, but I did need the liquid to keep going. My sense of euphoria was heightening and I was delighted to see many Indians having completed the race.

But my eyes were scanning for two individuals, in particular.

One, Derek, our tour guide, and after not much effort, I found him chatting with another official.

I walked up to him and showed him my Finisher medal. He seemed to remember me and mimicked me by twirling his non-existent moustache to give me that much-needed approval. I could see he was pleased with my finish.

While walking back to the runners' tent, I saw a runner hobbling his way back. I extended a hand to help him out; surprised to see that it was John. He had his one arm in a sling and injuries on his elbow and knees. The blood had dried, but it wasn't merely a scratch. It seemed he had a similar fall as mine and got the worst of it with a broken arm. As I was about to commiserate with his failed run, I saw the finisher's medal dangling on his neck, albeit of a different colour. He finished the race 30 minutes ahead of me and had earned the Bronze. I looked at him with my mouth agape.

BECOMING A RUNNER

Running for most of us seems a Daunting task. Something which came naturally to us in our younger years, seems herculean as we age. In our growing years, we tend to be more active but become sedentary as we attain adulthood and beyond. Whether in school or at home. Apparently even the reward system eventually disincentivises us away from sports and running. Our parent's generation was too busy putting food on our table for them to have disposable time or incomes. The case is different now. The current generation has ample of both and does not believe in delayed gratification. The now generation wants the action and the results now. Works for them in most aspects, except when results have a long haul involved. Actually, this seems to be a trait straddling all age groups now. Thankfully, India is poised for a health revolution with a plethora of events happening in the running circuit, the gates opened wide by the Mumbai Marathon started by Procam India. There has been a glut and even the 2020 pandemic has failed to press the brakes on the same. People are participating en-masse in virtual events organised by not just Indians but Global entities too.

This is good news for us as a Nation. Running can potentially make it a fitter country and help define our National character besides reduce our burgeoning Health bills.

Running has powers beyond physical fitness and transformation. It eventually transcends your mind and your "being." Healing the body and the soul. I have seen the sport being taken up for various reasons, from a strong need to look and feel fit to a statement of self determination and a focused activity to provide catharsis.

If this is your first foray, may I suggest a walk-run approach. Viz. run for some time and then walk, recovering your breath and your bearings.

Take It slow: As you take those first steps into becoming a runner, you may have BIG ambitions, but you need to start small, and allow yourself to discover the runner in you. For me, I started with Half Marathons, and took a good full 4 years to move to the Full Marathon. There is no magic formula to determine what is right for you. What may be right for me, may end up being too stiff a target for you or merely pedantic for you. The thumb rule is to ensure that you encounter minimal injuries. Yes, you will encounter a few; from pain in the heels to your knees screaming out.

But if there is consistent pain and discomfort, one of the three is not stacking up. Your stretching routine, a must for our contracted muscles to come to a relaxed state or your running form; a simple way is for some one to shoot a video for you while running. This will bring forth any unbalanced running gait you may have which might be putting undue stress on one or more of your body parts. And the last possibility is the volume and intensity of your running. Maybe you are pushing your body beyond its ability to stretch without causing significant injury or permanent damage. Remember, while it's running, it is not a race, especially with anyone else. The benchmark is for you to improve yourself and maybe in that process you will end up surpassing someone else; but that's not the core objective. Run for yourself, at your pace and craft your journey.

Structure your training: Running requires 3 key strengths. Your skeleto-muscular strength reflected in your endurance. Your ability to run longer distances. The second is your VO2 Max. Basically reflected in your ability to gulp in air/ oxygen, the capacity of your lungs. Last but not the least is Lactate threshold. As children we sometimes used to encounter being completely out of breath after running at high speeds and double over. This is nothing but lactic acid getting accumulated in your system. The same provides fuel for the energy burst, but insufficient disposal of the same can result in your coming to an abrupt halt. There are runs structured around the development of all three. Each one of them provides a holistic experience and makes a better runner out of you. Merely chugging miles will not cut it.

As per experts, too many of them end up being Junk miles and will have little or no effect on your running prowess. There may be days when you would just like to go and run unmindful of your pace or distance; please do so, they are great for the mind. Running helps in the production and release of serotonin to the brain, which is basically a mood lifter. Interestingly, if you try to do too much exercise, or feel forced into doing it, it may not have the right effect. Recognizing that you are choosing to exercise changes its neurochemical effect. That may be a result of your ancient instincts — the difference between running because you're hunting something and running because it's hunting you.

Confuse the mind & Body; Don't get stuck to one routine: spice it up. Keep the mind and Body engaged and responsive and not get into a pedantic rut. It is important to change the scenery every now and then. We may even get tired of eating our favourite food every day. The same can happen to your runs. Change the course and discover new vistas. Running requires all senses to be engaged. The eyes are as important as the rest of them. Merely being in an invigorating place can do wonders for the mind and body.

Rest Is important as is pushing yourself. They are the Yin & Yang of motion. The original concept of yin and yang came from the observation of nature and the environment. "Yin" originally referred to the shady side of a slope while "yang" referred to the sunny side. Later, this thinking was used in understanding other things, which occurred in pairs and had complementary and opposing characteristics in nature. Some examples include sky and earth, day and night, water, and fire, active and passive, male and female and so on. Running requires us to push our minds and bodies to its optimum level, for it to sustain those levels and to improve upon them requires healing, which comes in the form of rest and recuperation. The rest period allows the frayed and stressed tissue to heal and replenish the energy of the body. This does not mean that you remain inactive the rest of the days. Merely that you can indulge in complementary fitness exercises, ranging from Cycling or swimming to weight training. Do remember, the eventual objective is robust health of the mind & body.

Running is "Meditation in Motion." You need to focus on your form as much as you need to focus on the intensity and volume. While being a physical activity it is also an art form. Your mind and body need to be in balance. As such, it is important for you to be running with the right posture and possibly the correct stride. While no two runners will have the same form, you can still have a good form on a broad level. There are exceptions; but I have noticed them more in Elite athletes. For the common runner, a poor form can result in frequent injuries and down time. This can often result in a vicious cycle. One suggestion I often give to runners is to have an independent observer record their running and show them. An even better one will be to run in the gym on treadmill facing the mirror. Most gyms are equipped with reflective mirrors all around; to create a semblance of space, but also to cater to our vanity.

Your running shoes: Every runner will tell you with utmost passion about their favourite shoes. While some of it will be apocryphal, the merit of having the right type of running shoes cannot be stated enough. Many shops nowadays have treadmills to analyse your running gait. This helps determine how your foot lands and hence categorised as a pronator or a supinator. Both terms involve your gait and how your weight is distributed as you walk or run. Supination means that when you walk, your weight tends to be more on the outside of your foot. Pronation means that when you walk, your weight tends to be more on the inside of your foot. This will help you in identifying the right shoe type. The same will help in preventing long term injuries and provide efficiency to your run. Also, all things have a life span. Typically, shoes will be good for 500-700 kms. No matter how attached you are to them or how attractive they still look; they need to be discarded or mothballed. Whatever works for you.

Be adaptive; run alone and in groups. I started my journey by being a solo runner. My timings were such as also the fact that running had not taken up as a sport as it has in the recent past. Finding like minded people was no easy task. Also, the solitude I found in running in the fast paced Megapolis, Bombay was nectar for the soul. I really didn't feel the need to connect up with fellow runners. As I progressed to running Marathons, I felt the need for some guidance and information. I was discovering new things, from injuries to unwarranted fatigue and distress. I realised that merely pushing the body wasn't enough. I was also not conversant with nutrition usage and requirements. I believe that I could have compressed my journey if I had a peer group to discuss and share. There is immense learning which can happen in a group, and it accelerates the learning process. Eventually all of us will find our balance from intensity to volume or rest and Nutrition. But the basics still need to be learned, and group running is the best way forward. The Comrades Marathon requires a participant to walk around 15-20 kilometres given the steep inclines one encounters; I had to learn this. I was extremely uncomfortable walking in between a run as it would take away the momentum and I would feel tightness in my muscles. I started running more with my group of runners and found my body and mind adapting to the need. While group running is important to the running process, do not let go of your individuality and inner peace by letting go of solo running. Each has its benefits.

Don't let technology overtake you. Get your natural rhythm in place. Technology can be a big facilitator. But remember, the running still needs to be done. I was late in my adoption of technology, focusing more on the quantum of the running experience. The first Garmin (a GPS enabled watch) I incorporated was in my first Ultra Marathon, the Comrades run; albeit a borrowed one. Till then my mobile apps gave me a decent input on my pace and timings and to some extent the calories burnt. The use of technology can help you break up your run to analyses your strengths and weaknesses. It can tell you about cadence and pace. Cadence is merely the number of steps taken per minute. The ideal cadence is supposed to be 180. As we move forward our pace is determined by our cadence and stride length. Too low a cadence in a high speed implies that the stride is too long and prone to more wear and tear resulting in injuries. Too much cadence (very few runners will come in this bracket) implies insufficient usage of your quads and potentially lower speeds achieved. On the whole, if you are a recreational runner like me, cadence closer to 180 will help reduce wear and tear.

Incorporate Fitness, not just running into your life. My running journey took off when I finished my first half marathon more than a decade back. I undertook the running 3 to 4 months prior to the event and then moved to a sedentary mode. This continued for a couple of years before I incorporated running as a part of my lifestyle. It soon dawned on me that running in itself will not fulfil my fitness needs. My eating habits left a lot to be desired, as did my binge drinking on weekends. The realisation culminated over a period of time and I started incorporating more and more elements of a healthy living. Whether it was reduction/elimination of processed sugar, to moderation in eating and drinking. I also incorporated more of strength training and dallied in Yoga for some time. I was looking at having a healthy mind and body. The changes which were brought about were in my perspective towards life and the lifestyle I lead. I would urge runners to look at running as a means to evolving into holistic living and healthy lifestyles.

MY LEARNINGS AS A LEADER: THE TEN COMMANDMENTS

Self-awareness: This is one of the most basic requirements as a human being. But more so when you lead people. No matter what the domain, self-awareness is the starting point for any great leadership venture. It is not a static trait and keeps evolving as we do onion peeling of our personalities and go deeper into our motivations and fears. This can also be triggered by opening oneself to feedback and critique, including from team members and colleagues. It takes immense inner strength to put ourselves up for review. It also allows our team members to find us more relatable.

Know the ground: Almost all consumer facing organisations expect their trainees to spend time in the field, interacting with the customers and distributors. I was fortunate enough to have gone through a rigorous process, having joined an FMCG organisation with intensive distribution in the hinterland. This allowed me not merely a glimpse but first-hand knowledge of Bharat. While many of us may have grown up in non-metros, the flavour of the country lies in the rural setting. But it cannot be merely restricted to that, the need to understand the consumer needs to be paramount. I haven't seen too many leaders hit the field as their responsibility enhances. This allows a partial and potentially incorrect view of the consumer and the Business at Large. Knowing the consumer is as important as knowing the Business. Every time you change organisations, the first task at hand is to get a first-hand view of the consumer and customer.

You are as good as your team and Vice versa: The teams we lead change texture as time passes, attrition happens, and potentially new blood comes into the system. It also happens as we change organisations and take up different responsibilities. Constantly staying in touch with the quality of your team becomes paramount. The strategic plans and their execution are not driven by mathematics but rather by the execution rigour and the quality of implementation. Which is a function of you as a leader and the teams you lead. Not always do we get the option of hiring the team as per our standards/ requirements. Accordingly, the planning and objectives need to be calibrated. Be cognizant of that and avoid a copy paste solution as you move organisations.

They are looking for a leader, not a boss: Often in corporate parlance the term Boss is used for our supervisor and while our team members may be uncomfortable calling us by our first names, especially in hierarchical organisations, the fact that they are calling us Boss, does not imply that we need to act like one, or that they expect us to be one. Most team members are looking at a fair and supportive Leader.

Somebody they can look up to and who can guide them in difficult times. Demand the best from them, but ensure you are cognizant of the context before setting the expectation.

Empathy does not imply weakness: I have often observed Leaders failing to listen to the team member, or at the least giving him/her insufficient time to place/ share their thoughts. The underlying assumption being that they would come up with a litany of arguments and make the leader concede ground. This is merely a perception. By listening you are being privy to the thought process of the team member, and at the very least you end up getting an opportunity to appraise the potential of the resource. In the best-case scenario, it allows you to work constructively with the employee, focusing on her strengths and helping her carve out the blueprint for appropriate and timely action. Merely shouting orders does not imply strength rather displays an obstinate blinkered view and for the perceptive employee depicts an insecurity in the Leader.

Be firm but fair in your decision making: I have often had to take tough decisions. From taking punitive action, to terminating services of an employee, to having teams en-masse becoming redundant in the newer scheme of things. I have had at one time retrench people numbering 2,000 at one go, including asking 6 out of my 9 Vice Presidents. The one thing which salvaged this abhorrent situation was the transparency of the decision making. If we ensure standardisation of our actions, there will be few complaints and negligible heart burn, because no matter what, tough decisions will have to be taken.

Park your ego: Too many times I have seen Leaders confusing their role with their identity. It has been said that Power corrupts, and absolute power corrupts absolutely. In such cases it is important to remember that you are an instrument of implementation of the organisation, and not the organisation. You need to remember that organisations work on the principle of "Going concern Basis"; no matter whether you are there tomorrow or not; the organisation will continue to exist and thrive. You are holding a position; you are not the position. It is true you may end up exercising unfettered Power as long as you occupy that chair, but no sooner you end up vacating it, the list of your followers will Vanish. Their "loyalty" and association was to the Chair and not the chair holder. Park that ego and allow yourself to be one with the team; no matter how long you may have relinquished that chair; you will still be the centre of attention and adoration.

Evolve: It's a dynamic world. The world is changing, for the good and the bad. But most importantly; it's changing fast. For each one of us, adapting to newer situations is a prerequisite to be relevant in this technology age. The arbitrage in information was a big differentiation in bygone times. Reuters was set up in 1851 by Paul Julius Reuter, a German-born immigrant. He opened an office in the City of London which transmitted stock market quotations between London and Paris via the new Calais-Dover cable. The availability of information ahead of others was a competitive advantage which was milked to the core. Google and to some extent social media have made information access and timely availability redundant as a competitive advantage. As a leader, mere adoption or adaption will not suffice. You have to learn to read the Tea leaves and be at the forefront of defining that future. If you insist on being your previous Avatar, you will become obsolete before you even realise it and may be left with Tales to tell, prematurely retired sipping a glass of scotch.

Be a good listener: One of my favourite quotes comes is: “When you talk, you are only repeating what you already know. But if you listen, you may learn something new”: the Dalai Lama. Don’t fall in Love with your own voice. Reiteration of your learning will not hone it. Albeit, listening will give you information & Knowledge. More importantly, it will hone your ability to observe and get a better perspective.

Lead from the front: Do not expect your team to do what you are uncomfortable in doing. If they merely see you as someone passing instructions their faith in you will be nebulous at best, and their belief in the task will be perfunctory. A sense of purpose can only come in, if they have a role model to see and emulate. The Indian army has the highest casualty ratio of officers to soldiers, but also the highest success rate. To take up responsibility and to hold it firm in your grip requires courage. In my conversation with a Commanding Officer of a Special Forces unit; it came out very clearly that the officer needs to better at everything what he expects his team to do. Walk the talk.

EXCERPTS FROM "LEAP OF FAITH"

Yesterday, I experienced failure. Failure to achieve my dream.

I had been training for over 6 months to get the coveted Ironman title.

I am a good runner and a pretty decent athlete. Have run the Marathon in approx. 3 hours and 30 minutes. Have conquered Comrades back to back (for the non-runners, it's an iconic 89 km race in South Africa in the valley of 1000 hills to commemorate the fallen soldiers in WW I).

On the whole, I am reasonably fit, irrespective of my age.

I give 20-year-old runners a run for their money in sprints.

After having achieved reasonable success in my running endeavours, I switched to triathlons. With a rich grounding of 9 odd years of running, I have put more miles under my belt than the length and breadth of the country; that too, a couple of times over. I have also been a decent swimmer for more than a decade. That is to say, I can swim 50 laps without feeling out of breath.

I dabbled in cycling ever since I was a kid; moving onto brevets, a couple of years back. But in my heart, I have always been a runner. Rain or shine, good day or bad day, joy or sorrow, I have to run... It makes me feel alive, propelling me to live beyond just existing. When I run, I fly...I soar beyond my physical limitations. I experience each breath; I hear the sound of my heart beating to the rhythm of my legs. I experience each pore of my body...my cells come alive. My spirit soars and watches the world beneath with wonderment and joy.

I guess that in mind and body, I am still a teenager. I experience the unadulterated joy of experiencing things, every time, for the first time, and I experience pain as if my heart would break into a million pieces…

It's enough about me...let us move to the core of the story now.

So, my first Ironman was on the 27th of August, 2017, 5000 km away from home in a country I had only heard about… in France, an exotic and beautiful countryside. Endowed with the natural beauty of all kinds. Well, neither the beautiful women nor the enticing landscape was the decision-maker. It was the chance to swim in a lake as part of achieving the Ironman title. I had told you, I am a decent swimmer, not a great one. I enjoy the pools and swimming for hours; put me in open water and suddenly, I encounter amnesia as far as running is concerned... err... I meant swimming.

Unlike other sports, swimming changes texture the minute you move out of the pool. Your stamina, strength or form does not make much of a difference. Your mind does. It searches for hidden dangers in the depths of the lake or the ocean; one can encounter crocodiles in the arctic and sharks may spring up a surprise in the lake. There is a reason they say that your mind is the most creative of tools. It creates a world of its own. We experience it every day but usually, our mental realities are not too much out of sync from other people.

The Venn intersection is relatively high.

But the minute you enter the open water, it takes a journey into new worlds, especially for people who are not in love with the water. You may be swimming in a lake and feel like being in an adventure from **"20000 Leagues under the sea"**.

I am one of those travellers.

Knowing this, I decided to confront my fears by heading for a lake swim, about 40 km away from home, with friends who were planning for an Ironman in the near future. It meant getting up at an ungodly hour, driving for an hour and then hiking to the lake, 5 km away, on foot!

Cometh the hour, cometh the man: well not really, as the minute I waded into the water, I started hyperventilating, which meant simply that my swimming went for a toss. After a few minutes of familiarizing with the depths of the water and a friendly coaxing from my friends, I let my body free and started to swim. Voila, it worked! I could swim, even in a lake which was a million miles deep as far as I was concerned.

Having taken the baby steps, I decided to take the longer stretch in my stride or rather, my stroke, and I ended up swimming till the very end of the lake. Having sighted land, I could empathise with Christopher Columbus. The Promised Land was 10 feet away, and my friend was beckoning me to join him on the dry land. In my eagerness to wade across, I got onto a vertical position when reality hit me… the water was deeper than my tall 10-foot frame. I started going down, to be entangled with weeds which clamped me with their iron grip on my legs and more so, on my mind. To say that I panicked would be an understatement. My life flashed before me in the 2 dips I gulped water in. Thankfully, my vocal chords were in full flow to get the accompanying lifeguard to my assistance before I went down the 3rd time and possibly, the last time.

How life flashes across your eyes in a second is something to be experienced in order to be comprehended. I can say that I saw the light and came back, courtesy the 5 ft tall lifeguard with the heart of a lion.

Back on land, alive but not full of life, I decided to plunge again, after getting control of my bearings. No, I am not a sadist, but a rational guy, who understood that if I allow fear to make its home in the nook and cranny of my heart, it will be a difficult tenant to evict, if not an impossible one. I swam the way back, thankful to be alive and even happier that I had defeated fear, at least in this battle. In the back of my mind, I knew, there would be many more.

Having taken precautionary measures of the right safety equipment for my future swimming endeavours, I embarked on the physically and mentally arduous journey of becoming an Ironman.

After much research, I decided for Vichy France. The swim was in a lake; I was still unsure about trying my abilities in the open sea. The fickle nature of water gets significantly magnified in the sea. Further, the bike course would not sear my lungs too much; it had its own share of rolling hills but was not like the mountains of Switzerland, another enticing locale at par with the pristine beauty of France. The run was through the town of Vichy, along the banks of the river, interspersed with cafes and bars. A good reminder of what we would be enjoying post the event.

The rigmarole of early mornings and long workouts started.

An ironman training requires anywhere between 10 - 17 hours of intense training in a week. Besides training for the 3 sports viz. Swimming, Cycling and Running, you also work on strength training, especially for your core and legs. The weekdays are interspersed with various types of training. Merely covering more distance is not the solution. There is a fair bit of science involved and it reflects in the training regime. The longer workouts are kept for the weekend. This means that your Saturday and Sunday mornings are bestowed at the altar of God, IRONMAN! Ensuring that you not only become a social pariah but also get to miss out on some quality time with family, or so the wife tells me.

It's a different thing that many a time when you reach home after a 3-hour workout, the kids and wife are only waking up to a lazy Sunday morning and you are pumped up with adrenaline to take on the world; whereas for them, lifting an eyelid seems like a Herculean task.

The training schedule became a part of me, it was not something which I did; it was something I had become. An Ironman in the making. The transformation had commenced in earnest.

50 km bike rides were fun rides; a weekend typically implied a 20- 30 km run on Saturday followed by a 100-150 km bike ride on Sunday. In June, it transpired such that it was not only my body transforming but also my appearance; I had become a chameleon, that's what I deduced from the baffled looks of my family on one particular day after I walked in after a long *tandoori-burning* ride.

Swimming sessions became fortnightly visits to the charming lake; it had finally accepted me; besides alternate days of a couple of kilometres of swimming. These swims were in my apartment's building pool frequented by boisterous kids and aunties taking a leisurely walk in the pool, courtesy it had a depth of a mere 4 odd feet. Therefore, timings had to be managed so that I could do 100 laps in peace. *I was moving forward in my quest for inner peace.*

I believe, nothing teaches patience the way lap swimming does. With no scenery, no distractions, no music, you have absolutely nothing to do but swim. And trust me, it requires all your focus and more. Because, effort doesn't count as much as form does. It was as if this was the closest I had come to learning ballet. 'What Grace and poise,' I thought, although my Garmin thought otherwise. And yet, I could complete 4 km in an hour and forty minutes. Not bad, given that ironman cut-off was 2 hours and 20 minutes for the 3.8 km swim.

I was still struggling to up the ante on my bike speed. I was still riding an Aluminium bike whereas carbon bikes were in fashion. In this case, fashion had a functional advantage. It improved speed and reduced fatigue; the prerequisites, as on race day I would be running a full marathon after having my arse on a sliver of a saddle for about 7 hours, navigating 180 kilometres of the French countryside.

My prayers were answered; my wife was to attend a conference in San Francisco. She thought that the company trip was an all-expense paid one, till she saw the bill of the bike she was supposed to buy there and get back. And for what…so that her husband could finally proclaim what he always thought of himself – An Ironman?

New bike and a new man... suddenly I was flying... and for a change, Garmin agreed. My 100+ km rides became shorter and smoother.

The cross-training worked wonders for my running. But then, that was just the side dish.

The main course was to be served on 27th August in France.

Finally, the day arrived for heading to the exotic shores. 24 hours later, I was in the French countryside, asking myself a question, 'What am I doing here?' My 6-month intense training kept my mind from wandering too far. It would go to the depths of the lake and then bounce back. But there was interesting news headed my way, it was not a lake but a river. And the water was not cold enough for a wetsuit, which meant more effort, especially with the current. I would not have been able to take advantage of the highly buoyant wetsuit, which meant a longer swim.

By the time I reached the queue for starting the swim leg, I had achieved "inner peace", or so I thought. The minute I jumped into the water, the peace went to pieces as the cold water shook me like a rag doll and drew the breath out of me. At that moment, it was all about the control of the mind, and the body would have followed. Well, the mind kept meandering and I kept pulling it back. The tug of war continued for 800 odd meters when I finally tamed it and started my proper freestyle swim. I knew I had lost time but also knew that it was well within my capabilities to pull it back.

The first half of the swim was finished in 1 hour and 10 minutes, more than 20 minutes of my training swims, but I knew I had it under control as I was swimming with ease now, using all my training tips and pirouetting like a ballet dancer. I was confident that I would finish the 2nd half under 50 minutes with almost 20 minutes to spare for the cut-off.

And there I went, one stroke after the other, following a bright pink cap, unsure about the identity but sure about the gender. Good motivation. 2.5 km came and went. That is when something weird happened, I got a cramp in my left medial triceps, which never happened before, and I did not even know it could get cramped! This meant I had to be careful with how much strength I was applying and how my form was. I couldn't do breaststroke anymore to release my cough or get some breath, as it hurt a lot and I was unsure whether it would cramp enough for me to bail out and call the canoe. Soon enough I crossed the 3 km mark, but the pain did not go away. My younger son's earnest appeal in his voice kept prodding me to complete. It had done wonders for me in finishing Comrades the first time. I kept going on, not fast but steady, sure in my mind to finish it in the stipulated time. I had the swim in the bag as far as I was concerned.

The distance seemed to take its own sweet time to finish. After meandering a bit, I sighted the Promised Land. What a sight. Seemed like 100 metres to go.

Touchdown, and I walk up the ramp like Daniel Craig. Cool, calm and confident. Till I turn my wrist to check my watch.

The world fell apart, comprehension went for a drive and insanity prevailed. Garmin displayed a total time of 2:29:56 seconds. I had missed the cut-off by approximately 10 minutes.

Soon I heard my name on the loudspeaker, evoking hope that technology had failed, and I was still in the race.

Well, such endings rarely occur.

I was pronounced 10 minutes late.

I had never experienced such a level of calmness in me, as I walked away from the arena without a backward glance or a hope. I just kept walking and chanced to see my watch displaying that I had swum 4.56 km. 750 m more than the stipulated distance and I went numb. There was no thought, no regret and no hope but a calmness of acceptance.

I was not successful, but I was not a failure, either.